HORRID HENRY'S
FRIENDS AND ENEMIES

Meet HORRID HENRY
the laugh-out-loud
worldwide sensation!

★ Over 15 million copies sold in 27 countries and counting

★ # 1 chapter book series in the UK

★ Francesca Simon is the only American author to ever win the Galaxy British Book Awards Children's Book of the year (past winners include J. K. Rowling, Philip Pullman, and Eoin Colfer).

"A loveable bad boy."
—People

"Horrid Henry is a fabulous antihero…**a modern comic classic**." —*Guardian*

"**Wonderfully appealing to girls and boys alike**, a precious rarity at this age." —Judith Woods, *Times*

"The best children's comic writer."
—Amanda Craig, *Times*

"I love the Horrid Henry books by Francesca Simon. They have lots of funny bits in. And Henry always gets into trouble!" —Mia, age 6

"My two boys love this book, and **I have actually had tears running down my face and had to stop reading because of laughing so hard**." —T. Franklin, parent

"**Fine fare for beginning readers**, this clever book should find a ready audience." —*Booklist*

"**The angle here is spot-on, and reluctant readers will especially find lots to love about this early chapter book series**. Treat young readers to a book talk or read-aloud and watch Henry go flying off the shelf." —*Bulletin of the Center for Children's Books*

"I have tried out the Horrid Henry books with groups of children as a parent, as a baby-sitter, and as a teacher. **Children love to either hear them read aloud or to read them themselves**." —Danielle Hall, teacher

"A flicker of recognition must pass through most teachers and parents when they read Horrid Henry. **There's a tiny bit of him in all of us**." —Nancy Astee, *Child Education*

"**As a teacher…it's great to get a series of books my class loves**. They go mad for Horrid Henry." —teacher

"**Short, easy-to-read chapters will appeal to early readers, who will laugh at Henry's exaggerated antics and relate to his rambunctious personality**." —*School Library Journal*

"An absolutely fantastic series and surely a winner with all children. Long live Francesca Simon and her brilliant books! More, more please!"

—parent

"**Laugh-out-loud reading for both adults and children alike**." —parent

"**Henry's over-the-top behavior, the characters' snappy dialogue and Ross's hyperbolic line art will engage even the most reluctant readers—there's little reason to suspect the series won't conquer these shores as well**." —*Publishers Weekly*

Horrid Henry by Francesca Simon

HORRID HENRY'S

FRIENDS AND ENEMIES

Francesca Simon
Illustrated by Tony Ross

sourcebooks
jabberwocky

"Horrid Henry and Moody Margaret" and "Horrid Henry's Perfect Day" originally appeared in *Horrid Henry*, text © Francesca Simon 1994, illustrations © Tony Ross 1994

"Moody Margaret Moves In" and "Horrid Henry's Wedding" originally appeared in *Horrid Henry Tricks the Tooth Fairy*, text © Francesca Simon 1996, illustrations © Tony Ross 1996

"Horrid Henry and the Scary Sitter" originally appeared in *Horrid Henry and the Scary Sitter*, text © Francesca Simon 2002, illustrations © Tony Ross 2002

"Moody Margaret's Makeover" originally appeared in *Horrid Henry and the Abominable Snowman*, text © Francesca Simon 2007, illustrations © Tony Ross 2007

"Horrid Henry's Arch Enemy" originally appeared in *Horrid Henry and the Soccer Fiend*, text © Francesca Simon 2006, illustrations © Tony Ross 2006

"Perfect Peter's Revenge" originally appeared in *Horrid Henry and the Mega-Mean Time Machine*, text © Francesca Simon 2005, illustrations © Tony Ross 2005

"Horrid Henry's Stinkbomb" and "Horrid Henry's Sleepover" originally appeared in *Horrid Henry's Stinkbomb*, text © Francesca Simon 2002, illustrations © Tony Ross 2002

Jokes originally appeared in *Horrid Henry's Joke Book*, text © Francesca Simon 2004, illustrations © Tony Ross 2004

Cover and internal design © 2011 by Sourcebooks, Inc.
Sourcebooks and the colophon are registered trademarks of Sourcebooks, Inc.

Published by Sourcebooks Jabberwocky, an imprint of Sourcebooks, Inc.
P.O. Box 4410, Naperville, Illinois 60567-4410
(630) 961-3900
Fax: (630) 961-2168
www.jabberwockykids.com

Library of Congress Cataloging-in-Publication data is on file with the publisher.

Source of Production: Versa Press, East Peoria, Illinois, USA
Date of Production: May 2011
Run Number: 15100

Printed and bound in the United States of America.
VP 10 9 8 7 6 5 4 3 2 1

CONTENTS

HORRID HENRY
AND
MOODY MARGARET

....

"I'm Captain Hook!"

"No, I'm Captain Hook!"

"I'm Captain Hook," said Horrid
Henry.

"I'm Captain Hook," said Moody
Margaret.

They glared at each other.

"It's *my* hook," said Moody
Margaret.

Moody Margaret lived next door.

She did not like Horrid
Henry, and Horrid
Henry did not like
her. But when Rude
Ralph was busy, Clever
Clare had the flu, and
Sour Susan was her enemy,
Margaret would jump
over the wall to play
with Henry.

"Actually, it's my turn to be Hook
now," said Perfect Peter. "I've been
the prisoner for such a long time."

"Prisoner, be quiet!" said Henry.

"Prisoner, walk the plank!" said
Margaret.

"But I've walked it fourteen times
already," said Peter. "Please can I be
Hook now?"

"No, by thunder!" said Moody
Margaret. "Now out of my way,

2

worm!" And she swashbuckled across
the deck, waving her hook and
clutching her sword and dagger.

Margaret had eye patches and skulls
and crossbones and plumed hats and
cutlasses and sabers and snickersnees.

Henry had a stick.

This was why Henry played with
Margaret.

But Henry had to do terrible things
before playing with Margaret's

3

swords. Sometimes he had to sit and wait while she read a book. Sometimes he had to play "Moms and Dads" with her. Worst of all (please don't tell anyone), sometimes he had to be the baby.

Henry never knew what Margaret would do.

When he put a spider on her arm, Margaret laughed.

When he pulled her hair, Margaret pulled his harder.

When Henry screamed, Margaret would scream louder. Or she would sing. Or pretend not to hear.

Sometimes Margaret was fun. But most of the time she was a moody old grouch.

"I won't play if I can't be Hook," said Horrid Henry.

Margaret thought for a moment.

"We can both be Captain Hook,"
she said.

"But we only have one hook," said
Henry.

"Which I haven't played with yet,"
said Peter.

"BE QUIET, prisoner!" shouted
Margaret. "Mr. Smee, take him to jail."

"No," said Henry.

"You will get your reward, Mr. Smee," said the Captain, waving her hook.

Mr. Smee dragged the prisoner to the jail.

"If you're very quiet, prisoner, then you will be freed and you can be a pirate, too," said Captain Hook.

"Now give me the hook," said Mr. Smee.

The Captain reluctantly handed it over.

"Now I'm Captain Hook and you're Mr. Smee," shouted Henry. "I order everyone to walk the plank!"

"I'm sick of playing pirates," said Margaret. "Let's play something else."

Henry was furious. That was just like Moody Margaret.

"Well, I'm playing pirates," said
Henry.

"Well I'm not," said Margaret.
"Give me back my hook."

"No," said Henry.

Moody Margaret
opened her mouth
and screamed. Once
Margaret started
screaming she could
go on and on
and on.

Henry gave her
the hook.

Margaret smiled.

"I'm hungry,"
she said. "Got
anything good
to eat?"

Henry had three bags of chips and
seven chocolate cookies hidden in his

room, but he certainly wasn't going
to share them with Margaret.

"You can have a radish," said
Henry.

"What else?" said Margaret.

"A carrot," said Henry.

"What else?" said Margaret.

"Glop," said Henry.

"What's Glop?"

"Something special that only I can
make," said Henry.

"What's in it?" asked Margaret.

"That's a secret," said Henry.

"I bet it's yucky," said Margaret.

"Of course it's yucky," said
Henry.

"I can make the yuckiest Glop of
all," said Margaret.

"That's because you don't know
anything. No one can make yuckier
Glop than I can."

"I dare you to eat Glop," said Margaret.

"I double dare you back," said Henry. "Dares go first."

Margaret stood up very straight.

"All right," said Margaret. "Glop starts with snails and worms."

And she started poking under the bushes.

"Got one!" she shouted, holding up a fat snail.

"Now for some worms," said Margaret.

She got down on her hands and
knees and started digging a hole.

"You can't put anything from
outside into Glop," said Henry
quickly. "Only stuff in the kitchen."

Margaret looked at Henry.

"I thought we were making Glop,"
she said.

"We are," said Henry. "My way,
because it's *my* house."

Horrid Henry and Moody
Margaret went into the gleaming
white kitchen. Henry got out two
wooden mixing spoons and a giant
red bowl.

"I'll start," said Henry. He went
to the cupboard and opened the
doors wide.

"Oatmeal!" said Henry. And he
poured some into the bowl.

Margaret opened the fridge and

looked inside. She grabbed a small container.

"Soggy semolina!" shouted Margaret. Into the bowl it went.

"Coleslaw!"

"Spinach!"

"Coffee!"

"Yogurt!"

"Flour!"

"Vinegar!"

"Baked beans!"

"Mustard!"

"Peanut butter!"

"Moldy cheese!"

"Pepper!"

"Rotten oranges!"

"And ketchup!" shouted Henry.
He squirted in the ketchup until the
bottle was empty.

"Now, mix!" said Margaret.

Horrid Henry and Moody
Margaret grabbed hold of their
spoons with both hands. Then they
plunged the spoons into the Glop and
began to stir.

It was hard, heavy work.

Faster and faster, harder and harder
they stirred.

There was Glop on the ceiling.
There was Glop on the floor. There
was Glop on the clock, and Glop on
the door. Margaret's hair was covered
in Glop. So was Henry's face.

Margaret looked into the bowl. She
had never seen anything so yucky in
her life.

"It's ready," she said.

Horrid Henry and Moody
Margaret carried the Glop to the
table.

Then they sat down and stared at
the sloppy, slimy, sludgy, sticky,
smelly, gooey, gluey, gummy,
greasy, gloopy Glop.

"Right," said Henry. "Who's
going to eat some first?"

There was a very
long pause.

Henry looked at
Margaret.

Margaret looked
at Henry.

"Me," said
Margaret. "I'm not
scared."

She scooped up a
large spoonful and
stuffed it in her mouth.

Then she
swallowed. Her face
went pink and
purple and green.

"How does it
taste?" said Henry.

"Good," said
Margaret, trying not
to choke.

"Have some more
then," said Henry.

"Your turn first,"
said Margaret.

Henry sat for a moment and looked at the Glop.

"My mom doesn't like me to eat between meals," said Henry.

"HENRY!" hissed Moody Margaret.

Henry took a tiny spoonful.

"More!" said Margaret.

Henry took a tiny bit more. The Glop wobbled lumpily on his spoon. It looked like...Henry did not want to think about what it looked like.

He closed his eyes and brought the spoon to his mouth.

"Ummm, yummm," said Henry.

"You didn't eat any," said Margaret. "That's not fair."

She scooped up some Glop and...

I dread to think what would have

happened next, if they had not been
interrupted.

"Can I come out now?" called a
small voice from outside. "It's my
turn to be Hook."

Horrid Henry had forgotten all
about Perfect Peter.

"OK," shouted Henry.

Peter came to the door.

"I'm hungry," he said.

"Come in, Peter," said Henry
sweetly. "Your dinner is on the table."

MOODY MARGARET MOVES IN

....

Mom was on the phone.

"Of course we'd be delighted to have Margaret," she said. "It will be no trouble at all."

Henry stopped breaking the tails off Peter's plastic horses.

"WHAT?" he howled.

"Shh, Henry," said Mom. "No, no," she added. "Henry is delighted, too. See you Friday."

"What's going on?" said Henry.

"Margaret is coming to stay while her parents go on vacation," said Mom.

Henry was speechless with horror.

"She's going to stay…here?"

"Yes," said Mom.

"How long?" said Henry.

"Two weeks," said Mom brightly.

Horrid Henry could not stand Moody Margaret for more than two minutes.

"Two weeks?" he said. "I'll run away! I'll lock her out of the house, I'll pull her hair out, I'll…"

"Don't be horrid, Henry," said Mom. "Margaret's a lovely girl and I'm sure we'll have fun."

"No we won't," said Henry. "Not with that moody old grouch."

"I'll have fun," said Perfect Peter. "I love having guests."

"She's not sleeping in my room," said Horrid Henry. "She can sleep in the basement."

"No," said Mom. "You'll move into

Peter's room and let Margaret have your
bed."

Horrid Henry opened his mouth
to scream, but only a rasping sound
came out. He was so appalled he could
only gasp.

"Give…up…my…room!" he choked.
"To…Margaret?"

Margaret spying on his treasures,
sleeping in *his* bed, playing with *his*
toys while he had to share a room
with Peter…

"No!" howled Henry. He fell on the
floor and screamed. "NO!!"

"I don't mind giving up my bed for a
guest," said Perfect Peter. "It's the polite
thing to do. Guests come first."

Henry stopped howling just long
enough to kick Peter.

"Owww!" screamed Peter. He burst
into tears, "Mom!"

"Henry!" yelled Mom. "You horrid boy! Say sorry to Peter."

"She's not coming!" shrieked Henry. "And that's final."

"Go to your room!" yelled Mom.

Moody Margaret arrived at Henry's house with her parents, four suitcases, seven boxes of toys, two pillows, and a trumpet.

"Margaret won't be any trouble," said her mom. "She's always polite, eats everything, and never complains. Isn't that right, Precious?"

"Yes," said Margaret.

"Margaret's no fusspot," said her dad. "She's good as gold, aren't you, Precious?"

"Yes," said Margaret.

"Have a lovely vacation," said Mom.

"We will," said Margaret's parents.

The door slammed behind them.

Moody Margaret marched into the living room and swept a finger across the mantel.

"It's not very clean, is it?" she said. "You'd never find so much dust at *my* house."

"Oh," said Dad.

"A little dust never hurt anyone," said Mom.

"I'm allergic," said Margaret. "One whiff of dust and I start to…sn…sn…ACHOOO!" she sneezed.

"We'll clean up right away," said Mom.

Dad mopped.

Mom swept.

Peter dusted.

Henry vacuumed.

Margaret directed.

"Henry, you've missed a big dust ball right there," said Margaret, pointing under the sofa.

Horrid Henry vacuumed as far away from the dust as possible.

"Not there, here!" said Margaret.

Henry aimed the vacuum at Margaret. He was a fire-breathing dragon burning his prey to a crisp.

"Help!" shrieked Margaret.

"Henry!" said Dad.

"Don't be horrid," said Mom.

"I think Henry should be punished," said Margaret. "I think he should be locked in his bedroom for three weeks."

"I don't have a bedroom to be locked up in 'cause you're in it," said Henry. He glared at Margaret.

Margaret glared back.

"I'm the guest, Henry, so you'd better be polite," hissed Margaret.

"Of course he'll be polite," said Mom. "Don't worry, Margaret. Any trouble, you come straight to me."

"Thank you," said Moody Margaret, smiling. "I will. I'm hungry," she added.

"Why isn't supper ready?"

"It will be soon," said Dad.

"But I *always* eat at six o'clock," said Margaret, "I want to eat NOW."

"All right," said Dad.

Horrid Henry and Moody Margaret dashed for the seat facing the garden. Margaret got there first. Henry shoved her off. Then Margaret shoved him off.

Thud. Henry landed on the floor.

"Ouch," said Henry.

"Let the guest have the chair," said Dad.

"But that's my chair," said Henry. "That's where I *always* sit."

"Have my chair, Margaret," said Perfect Peter. "I don't mind."

"I want to sit here," said Moody Margaret. "I'm the guest so I decide."

Horrid Henry dragged himself around the table and sat next to Peter.

"OUCH!" shrieked Margaret. "Henry kicked me!"

"No I didn't," said Henry, outraged.

"Stop it, Henry," said Mom. "That's no way to treat a guest."

Henry stuck out his tongue at
Margaret. Moody Margaret stuck out her
tongue even further, then stomped on
his foot.

"OUCH!" shrieked Henry. "Margaret
kicked me!"

Moody Margaret gasped. "Oh I'm ever

so sorry, Henry," she said sweetly. "It was an accident. Silly me. I didn't mean to, really I didn't."

Dad brought the food to the table.

"What's *that?*" asked Margaret.

"Baked beans, corn on the cob, and chicken," said Dad.

"I don't like baked beans," said Margaret. "And I like my corn *off* the cob."

Mom scraped the corn off the cob.

"No, put the corn on a separate plate!" shrieked Margaret. "I don't like vegetables touching my meat."

Dad got out the pirate plate, the duck plate, and the "Happy birthday, Peter" plate.

"I want the pirate plate," said Margaret, snatching it.

"I want the pirate plate," said Henry, snatching it back.

"I don't mind which plate I get," said Perfect Peter. "A plate's a plate."

"No it isn't!" shouted Henry.

"I'm the guest," shouted Margaret. "I get to choose."

"Give her the pirate plate, Henry," said Dad.

"It's not fair," said Henry, glaring at his plate decorated with little ducks.

"She's the guest," said Mom.

"So?" said Henry. Wasn't there an ancient Greek who stretched all his guests on an iron bed if they were too short or lopped off their heads and feet if they were too long? That guy sure knew how to deal with horrible guests like Moody Margaret.

"Yuck," said Margaret, spitting out a mouthful of chicken. "You put salt on it!"

"Only a little," said Dad.

"I never eat salt," said Moody
Margaret. "It's not good for me. And I
always have peas at *my* house."

"We'll get some tomorrow," said Mom.

★ ★ ★

Peter lay asleep in the top bunk. Horrid
Henry sat listening by the door. He'd
scattered crumbs all over Margaret's bed.
He couldn't wait to hear her scream.

But there wasn't a sound coming from
Henry's room, where Margaret the
Invader lay. Henry couldn't understand it.

Sadly, he climbed into (oh, the shame of
it) the *bottom* bunk. Then he screamed.

His bed was filled with jam, crumbs,
and something squishy squashy and
horrible.

"Go to sleep, Henry!" shouted Dad.

That Margaret! He'd booby trap the
room, cut up her doll's clothes, paint her
face purple...Henry smiled grimly. Oh
yes, he'd show Moody Margaret.

Mom and Dad sat in the living room
watching TV.

Moody Margaret appeared on the stairs.

33

"I can't sleep with that noise," she said.

Mom and Dad looked at each other.

"We are watching very quietly, dear," said Mom.

"But I can't sleep if there's any noise in the house," said Margaret. "I have very sensitive ears."

Mom turned off the TV and picked up her knitting needles.

Click click click.

Margaret reappeared.

"I can't sleep with that clicking noise," she said.

"All right," said Mom. She sighed a little.

"And it's cold in my bedroom," said Moody Margaret.

Mom turned up the heat.

Margaret reappeared.

"Now it's too hot," said Moody Margaret.

Dad turned down the heat.

"My room smells funny," said Margaret.

"My bed is too hard," said Margaret.

"My room is too stuffy," said Margaret.

"My room is too light," said Margaret.

"Good night, Margaret," said Mom.

"How many more days is she staying?" said Dad.

Mom looked at the calendar.

"Only thirteen," said Mom.

Dad hid his face in his hands.

"I don't know if I can live that long," said Dad.

TOOTA TOOT. Mom blasted out of bed.

TOOTA TOOT. Dad blasted out of bed.

TOOTA TOOT. TOOTA TOOT.

TOOTA TOOT TOOT TOOT.

Henry and Peter blasted out of bed.

Margaret marched down the hall, playing her trumpet.

TOOTA TOOT. TOOTA TOOT.

TOOTA TOOT TOOT TOOT
TOOT.

"Margaret, would you mind playing your trumpet a little later?" said Dad, clutching his ears. "It's six o'clock in the morning."

"That's when I wake up," said Margaret.

"Could you play a little more softly?" said Mom.

"But I have to practice," said Moody Margaret.

The trumpet blared through the house. TOOT TOOT TOOT.

Horrid Henry turned on his radio. BOOM BOOM BOOM.

Margaret played her trumpet louder. TOOT! TOOT! TOOT!

Henry blasted his radio as loud as he could.

BOOM! BOOM! BOOM!

"Henry!" shrieked Mom.

"Turn that down!" bellowed Dad.

"Quiet!" screamed Margaret. "I can't practice with all this noise." She put down her trumpet. "And I'm hungry. Where's my breakfast?"

"We have breakfast at eight," said Mom.

"But I want breakfast now," said Margaret.

Mom had had enough.

"No," said Mom firmly. "We eat at eight."

Margaret opened her mouth and screamed. No one could scream as long, or as loud, as Moody Margaret.

Her piercing screams echoed through the house.

"All right," said Mom. She knew when she was beaten. "We'll eat now."

* * *

Henry's diary.

Monday I put crumbs in Margaret's bed. She put jam, crusts, and slugs in mine.

Tuesday Margaret found my secret cookies and chips and ate every single one.

Wednesday I can't play cd's at night because it disturbs grumpy-face Margaret.

Thursday I can't sing because it disturbs frog-face.

Friday I can't breathe because it disturbs misery-guts.

Saturday

I can stand it No Longer

That night, when everyone was asleep, Horrid Henry crept into the living room and picked up the phone.

"I'd like to leave a message," he whispered.

Bang bang bang bang bang.

Ding dong! Ding dong! Ding dong!

Henry sat up in bed.

Someone was banging on the front door and ringing the bell.

"Who could that be at this time of night?" yawned Mom.

Dad peeked through the window then opened the door.

"Where's my baby?" shouted Margaret's mom.

"Where's my baby?" shouted Margaret's dad.

"Upstairs," said Mom. "Where else?"

"What's happened to her?" shrieked Margaret's mom.

"We got here as quick as we could!" shrieked Margaret's dad.

Mom and Dad looked at each other. What was going on?

"She's fine," said Mom.

Margaret's mom and dad looked at each other. What was going on?

"But the message said it was an emergency and to come at once," said Margaret's mom.

"We cut short our vacation," said Margaret's dad.

"What message?" said Mom.

"What's going on? I can't sleep with all this noise," said Moody Margaret.

Margaret and her parents had gone home.

"What a terrible mix-up," said Mom.

"Such a shame they cut short their vacation," said Dad.

"Still…" said Mom. She looked at Dad.

"Hmmm," said Dad.

"You don't think that Henry…" said Mom.

"Not even Henry could do something so horrid," said Dad.

Mom frowned.

"Henry!" said Mom.

Henry continued sticking Peter's stamps together.

"Yeah?"

"Do you know anything about a message?"

"Me?" said Henry.

"You," said Mom.

"No," said Henry. "It's a mystery."

"That's a lie, Henry," said Perfect Peter.

"Is not," said Henry.

"Is too," said Peter. "I heard you on the phone."

Henry lunged at Peter. He was a mad bull charging the matador.

"YOWWWWW," shrieked Peter.

Henry stopped. He was in for it now. No allowance for a year. No candy for ten years. No TV ever.

Henry squared his shoulders and waited for his punishment.

Dad put his feet up.

"That was a terrible thing to do," said Dad.

Mom turned on the TV.

"Go to your room," said Mom.

Henry bounced upstairs. Your room. Sweeter words were never spoken.

HORRID HENRY AND THE SCARY SITTER

"No way!" shrieked Tetchy Tess, slamming down the phone.

"No way!" shrieked Crabby Chris, slamming down the phone.

"No way!" shrieked Angry Anna. "What do you think I am, crazy?"

Even Mellow Martin said he was busy.

Mom hung up the phone and groaned.

It wasn't easy finding someone to babysit more than once for Horrid Henry. When Tetchy Tess came, Henry flooded the bathroom. When Crabby Chris came he hid her homework and "accidentally" poured red grape juice down the front of her new white jeans. And when Angry Anna came, Henry— no, it's too dreadful. Suffice it to say that Anna ran screaming from the house and Henry's parents had to come home early.

Horrid Henry hated babysitters. He wasn't a baby. He didn't want to be sat on. Why should he be nice to some ugly, stuck-up, bossy teenager who'd hog the TV and pig out on Henry's cookies? Parents should just stay at home where they belonged, thought Horrid Henry.

And now it looked like they would have to. Ha! His parents were mean and horrible, but he'd had a lot of practice managing them. Babysitters were unpredictable. Babysitters were hard work. And by the time you'd broken them in and shown them who was boss, for some reason they didn't want to come any more. The good babysitters let you

stay up all night and eat candy until you
were sick. Sadly, Horrid Henry never got
one of those.

"We have to find a babysitter," wailed
Mom. "The party is tomorrow night.
I've tried everyone. Who else is there?"

"There's got to be someone," said
Dad. "Think!"

Mom thought.

Dad thought.

"What about Rebecca?" said Dad.

Horrid Henry's heart missed a beat.
He stopped drawing mustaches on
Perfect Peter's school pictures. Maybe

he'd heard wrong. Oh please, not Rebecca! Not—Rabid Rebecca!

"Who did you say?" asked Henry. His voice quavered.

"You heard me," said Dad. "Rebecca."

"NO!" screamed Henry. "She's horrible!"

"She's not horrible," said Dad. "She's just—strict."

"There's no one else," said Mom grimly. "I'll call Rebecca."

"She's a monster!" wailed Henry. "She made Ralph go to bed at six o'clock!"

"I like going to bed at six o'clock," said Perfect Peter. "After all, growing children need their rest."

Horrid Henry growled and attacked. He was the Creature from the Black

Lagoon, dragging the foolish mortal down to a watery grave.

"AAAEEEEE!" squealed Peter. "Henry pulled my hair."

"Stop being horrid, Henry!" said Dad. "Mom's on the phone."

Henry prayed. Maybe she'd be busy. Maybe she'd say no. Maybe she'd be dead. He'd heard all about Rebecca. She'd made Tough Toby get in his pajamas at five o'clock *and* do all his homework. She'd unplugged Dizzy Dave's computer.

She'd made Moody Margaret wash
the floor. No doubt about it, Rabid
Rebecca was the toughest teen in town.

Henry lay on the rug and howled.
Mom shouted into the phone.

"You can! That's great, Rebecca. No,
that's just the TV—sorry for the noise.
See you tomorrow."

"NOOOOOOOOO!" wailed Henry.

Ding dong.

"I'll get it!" said Perfect Peter. He
skipped to the door.

Henry flung himself on the carpet.

"I DON'T WANT TO HAVE A
BABYSITTER!" he wailed.

The door opened. In walked the biggest,
meanest, ugliest, nastiest-looking girl
Henry had ever seen. Her arms were
enormous. Her head was enormous.
Her teeth were enormous. She looked
like she ate elephants for breakfast,

 crocodiles for lunch, and snacked on toddlers.

"What have you got to eat?" snarled Rabid Rebecca.

Dad took a step back. "Help yourself to anything in the fridge," said Dad.

"Don't worry, I will," said Rebecca.

"GO HOME, YOU WITCH!" howled Henry.

"Bedtime is nine o'clock," shouted Dad, trying to be heard above Henry's screams. He edged his way carefully past Rebecca, jumped over Henry, then dashed out the front door.

"I DON'T WANT TO HAVE A BABYSITTER!" shrieked Henry.

"Be good, Henry," said Mom weakly. She stepped over Henry, then escaped from the house.

The door closed.

Horrid Henry was alone in the house with Rabid Rebecca.

He glared at Rebecca.

Rebecca glared at him.

"I've heard all about you, you little creep," growled Rebecca. "No one bothers me when I'm babysitting."

Horrid Henry stopped screaming.

"Oh yeah," said Horrid Henry.
"We'll see about that."

Rabid Rebecca bared her fangs. Henry
recoiled. Perhaps I'd better keep out of
her way, he thought, then slipped into
the living room and turned on the TV.

Ahh, *Mutant Max*. Hurray! How bad
could life be when a great program
like *Mutant Max* was on? He'd annoy
Rebecca as soon as it was over.

Rebecca stomped into the room and snatched the remote.

ZAP!

DA DOO, DA DOO DA, DA DOO DA DOO DA, tangoed some horrible spangled dancers.

"Hey," said Henry. "I'm watching *Mutant Max*."

"Tough," said Rebecca. "*I'm* watching ballroom dancing."

Snatch!

Horrid Henry grabbed the clicker.

ZAP!

"And it's mutants, mutants, mut—"

Snatch!

Zap!

DA DOO, DA DOO DA, DA DOO
DA DOO DA.

DOO, DA DOO DA, DA DOO DA
DOO DA.

Horrid Henry tangoed around the
room, gliding and sliding.

"Stop it," muttered Rebecca.

Henry shimmied back and forth in
front of the TV, blocking her view and
singing along as loudly as he could.

"DA DOO, DA DOO DA," warbled
Henry.

"I'm warning you," hissed Rebecca.

Perfect Peter walked in. He had
already put on his blue bunny pajamas,
brushed his teeth, and combed his hair.
He held a game of Chinese Checkers in
his hand.

"Rebecca, will you play a game with
me before I go to bed?" asked Peter.

"NO!" roared Rebecca. "I'm trying
to watch TV. Shut up and go away."

Perfect Peter leaped back.

"But I thought—since I was all ready for bed—" he stammered.

"I've got better things to do than to play with you," snarled Rebecca. "Now go to bed this minute, both of you."

"But it's not my bedtime for hours," protested Henry. "I want to watch *Mutant Max*."

"Or mine," said Perfect Peter timidly. "There's this nature program—"

"GO!" howled Rebecca.

"NO!" howled Henry.

"RAAAAA!" roared Rabid Rebecca.

Horrid Henry did not know how it happened. It was as if fiery dragon's breath had blasted him upstairs. Somehow, he was

in his pajamas, in bed, and it was only
seven o'clock.

Rabid Rebecca switched off the light.
"Don't even think of moving from
that bed," she hissed. "If I see you, or
hear you, or even smell you, you'll be
sorry you were born.
I'll stay downstairs,
you stay upstairs,
and that way no
one will get hurt."
Then she marched
out of the room and
slammed the door.

Horrid Henry was so shocked he
could not move. He, Horrid Henry,
the bulldozer of babysitters, the terror
of teachers, the bully of brothers, was in
bed, lights out, at seven o'clock.

Seven o'clock! Two whole hours
before his bedtime! This was an
outrage! He could hear Moody Margaret

shrieking next door. He could hear
Toddler Tom zooming around on his
tricycle. No one went to bed at seven
o'clock. Not even toddlers!

Worst of all, he was thirsty. So what
if she told me to stay in bed, thought
Horrid Henry. I'm thirsty. I'm going to
go downstairs and get myself a glass of
water. It's my house and I'll do what
I want.

Horrid Henry did not move.

I'm dying of thirst here, thought
Henry. Mom and Dad will come home

and I'll be a dried out old stick insect,
and boy will she be in trouble.

Horrid Henry still did not move.

Go on, feet, urged Henry, let's just
step on down and get a little ol' glass of
water. So what if that scary sitter said
he had to stay in bed.
What could she do
to him?

She could chop
off my head and
bounce it down
the stairs,
thought Henry.

Eeek.

Well, let her try.

Horrid Henry remembered who
he was. The boy who'd sent teachers
shrieking from the classroom. The boy
who'd destroyed the Demon Dinner
Lady. The boy who had run away from
home and almost reached the Congo.

I will get up and get a drink of water, he thought.

Sneak. Sneak. Sneak.

Horrid Henry crept to the bedroom door.

Slowly he opened it a crack.

Creak. Then slowly, slowly, he opened the door a bit more and slipped out.

ARGHHHHHH!

There was Rabid Rebecca sitting at the top of the stairs.

It's a trap, thought Henry. She was lying in wait for me. I'm dead, I'm finished, they'll find my bones in the morning.

Horrid Henry dashed back inside his room and awaited his doom.

Silence.

What was going on? Why hadn't Rebecca torn him apart limb from limb?

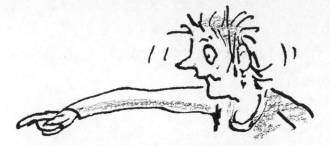

Horrid Henry opened his door a fraction and peeped out.

Rabid Rebecca was still sitting huddled at the top of the stairs. She did not move. Her eyes were fixed straight ahead.

"Spi–spi–spider," she whispered. She pointed at a big, hairy spider in front of her with a trembling hand.

"It's huge," said Henry. "Really hairy and horrible and wriggly and—"

"STOP!" squealed Rebecca. "Help me, Henry," she begged.

Horrid Henry was not the fearless leader of a pirate gang for nothing.

"If I risk my life and get rid of the spider, can I watch *Mutant Max*?" asked Henry.

"Yes," said Rebecca.

"And stay up till my parents come home?"

"Yes," said Rebecca.

"And eat all the ice cream in the fridge?"

"YES!" shrieked Rebecca. "Just get rid of that—that—"

"Deal," said Horrid Henry.

He dashed to his room and grabbed a jar.

Rabid Rebecca hid her eyes as Horrid Henry scooped up the spider. What a beauty!

"It's gone," said Henry.

Rebecca opened her beady red eyes.

"Right, back to bed, you little brat!"

"What?" said Henry.

"Bed. Now!" screeched Rebecca.

"But we agreed…" said Henry.

"Tough," said Rebecca. "That was then."

"Traitor," said Henry.

He whipped out the spider jar from behind his back and unscrewed the lid.

"On guard!" he said.

"AAEEEE!" whimpered Rebecca.

Horrid Henry advanced menacingly toward her.

"NOOOOOOO!" wailed Rebecca, stepping back.

"Now get in that room and stay there," ordered Henry. "Or else."

Rabid Rebecca skedaddled into the bathroom and locked the door.

"If I see you or hear you or even smell you, you'll be sorry you were born," said Henry.

"I already am," said Rabid Rebecca.

Horrid Henry spent a lovely evening in front of the TV. He watched scary movies. He ate ice cream and candy and cookies and chips until he could stuff no more in.

Vroom vroom.

Oops. Parents home.

Horrid Henry dashed upstairs and leaped into bed just as the front door opened.

Mom and Dad looked around the living room, littered with candy wrappers, cookie crumbs, and ice cream cartons.

"You did tell her to help herself," said Mom.

"Still," said Dad. "What a pig."

"Never mind," said Mom brightly, "at least she managed to get Henry to bed. That's a first."

Rabid Rebecca staggered into the room.

"Did you get enough to eat?" said Dad.

"No," said Rabid Rebecca.

"Oh," said Dad.

"Was everything all right?" asked Mom.

Rebecca looked at her.

"Can I go now?" said Rebecca.

"Any chance you could babysit on Saturday?" asked Dad hopefully.

"What do you think I am, crazy?" shrieked Rebecca.

SLAM!

Upstairs, Horrid Henry groaned.

Rats. It was so unfair. Just when he had a babysitter beautifully trained, for some reason they wouldn't come back.

MOODY MARGARET'S MAKEOVER

....

"Watch out, Gurinder! You're smearing your nail polish," screeched Moody Margaret. "Violet! Don't touch your face—you're spoiling all my hard work. Susan! Sit still."

"I am sitting still," said Sour Susan. "Stop pulling my hair."

"I'm not pulling your hair," hissed Margaret. "I'm styling it."

"Ouch!" squealed Susan. "You're hurting me."

"I am not, crybaby."

"I'm not a crybaby," howled Susan.
Moody Margaret sighed loudly.

"Not everyone can be naturally beautiful like me. Some people"—she glared at Susan—"have to work at it."

"You're not beautiful," said Sour Susan, snorting.

"I am too," said Margaret, primping herself.

"Are not," said Susan. "On the ugly scale of 1 to 10, with 1 being the ugliest, wartiest toad, you're a 2."

"Huh!" said Margaret. "Well, *you're* so ugly you're minus 1. They don't have an ugly enough scale for *you*."

"I want my money back!" shrieked Susan.

"No way!" shrieked Margaret. "Now sit down and shut up."

Across the wall in the next garden, deep inside the branches hiding the top secret entrance of the Purple Hand fort, a master spy pricked up his ears.

Money? Had he heard the word *money?*

What was going on next door?

Horrid Henry zipped out of his fort and dashed to the low wall separating his yard from Margaret's. Then he stared. And stared some more. He'd seen many weird things in his life. But nothing as weird as this.

Moody Margaret, Sour Susan, Lazy Linda, Vain Violet, and Gorgeous Gurinder were sitting in Margaret's garden. Susan had rollers tangling her pink hair. Violet had blue mascara all over her face. Linda was covered in gold glitter. There was spilled nail polish, face powder, and broken lipstick all over Margaret's patio.

Horrid Henry burst out laughing.

"Are you playing clowns?" said Henry.

"Huh, shows how much *you* know, Henry," said Margaret. "*I'm* doing makeovers."

"What's that?" said Henry.

"It's when you change how people look, dummy," said Margaret.

"I knew that," lied Henry. "I just wanted to see if you did."

Margaret waved a flyer in his face.

MARGARET'S
MAGNIFICENT MAKEOVERS!

I can make you beautiful!

Yes, even YOU.

No one too old or too ugly.

Only $1 for a new you!!!!!

Hurry!
Special offer ends soon!!!!!!!!!!!

Makeovers? Makeovers? What an incredibly stupid idea. Who'd pay to have a moody old grouch like Margaret smear gunk all over their face? Ha! No one.

Horrid Henry started laughing and pointing.

Vain Violet looked like a demon with red and blue and purple gloop all over her face. Gorgeous Gurinder looked as if a paint pot had been poured down her

cheeks. Linda's hair looked as if she'd
been struck by lightning.

But Violet wasn't screaming and
yanking Margaret's hair out. Instead she
handed Margaret—*money*.

"Thanks, Margaret, I look amazing,"
said Vain Violet,
admiring herself in
the mirror. Henry
waited for the
mirror
to crack.

It didn't.

"Thanks, Margaret," said Gurinder. "I look so fantastic I hardly recognize myself." And she also handed Margaret a dollar.

Two whole dollars? Were they mad?

"Are you getting ready for the Monster's Ball?" jeered Henry.

"Shut up, Henry," said Vain Violet.

"Shut up, Henry," said Gorgeous Gurinder.

"You're just jealous because I'm going to be rich and you're not," said Margaret. "Nah nah ne nah nah."

"Why don't we give Henry a makeover?" said Violet.

"Good idea," said Moody Margaret. "He could sure use one."

"Yeah," said Sour Susan.

Horrid Henry took a step back.

Margaret advanced toward him wielding nail polish and a hairbrush. Violet followed clutching a lipstick, hair dye, and other instruments of torture.

Yikes! Horrid Henry dashed back to the safety of his fort as fast as he could, trying to ignore the horrible, cackling laughter.

He sat on his Purple Hand throne and scarfed some extra tasty chocolate cookies from the secret stash he'd swiped from Margaret yesterday. Makeovers! Ha! How dumb could you get? Trust a pea-brained grouch like Margaret to come up with such a stupid idea. Who in their right mind would want a makeover?

On the other hand...

Horrid Henry had actually seen

Margaret being paid. And good money, too, just for smearing some colored gunk onto people's faces and yanking their hair around.

Hmmmm.

Horrid Henry started to think. Maybe Margaret *did* have a little eensy-weensy teeny-tiny bit of a good idea. And,  naturally, anything she could do, Henry could do much, much better. Margaret obviously didn't know the first thing about makeovers, so why should *she* make all that money, thought Horrid Henry indignantly. He'd steal—no, *borrow*—her idea and do it better. Much much better. He'd make people look *really* fantastic.

Henry's Makeovers. Henry's Marvelous Makeovers. Henry's Miraculous Makeovers. He'd be rich! With some false teeth and a red marker he could turn Miss Battle-Axe into a vampire. Mrs. Oddbod could be a perfect Dracula. And wouldn't Stuck-Up Steve be improved after a short visit from the Makeover Magician? Even Aunt Ruby wouldn't recognize him when Henry had finished. Tee-hee.

First, he needed supplies. That was easy: Mom had tons of gunk for smearing all over her face. And if he ran out he could always use crayons and glue.

Horrid Henry dashed to the bathroom
and helped himself to a few handfuls
of Mom's makeup. What on earth
did she need all this stuff for? thought
Henry, piling it into
a bag. About time
someone
cleared out
this drawer.
Then he wrote
a few flyers.

Horrid Henry, Makeover Magician,
was ready for business.

All he needed were some customers.
Preferably rich, ugly customers. Now,
where could he find some of those?

Henry strolled into the living room.
Dad was reading on the sofa. Mom was
working at the computer.

Horrid Henry looked at his aged,
wrinkly, boring old parents. Bleeeccch!

Boy, could they be improved, thought

Henry. How could he tactfully persuade these potential customers that they needed his help—fast?

"Mom," said Henry, "you know Great-Aunt Greta?"

"Yes," said Mom.

"Well, you're starting to look just like her."

"What?" said Mom.

"Yup," said Horrid Henry, "old and ugly. Except—" he peered at her, "you have more wrinkles."

"*What?*" squeaked Mom.

"And Dad looks like a gargoyle," said Henry.

"Huh?" said Dad.

"Only scarier," said Henry. "But don't worry, I can help."

"Oh really?" said Mom.

"Oh really?" said Dad.

"Yeah," said Henry, "I'm doing makeovers." He handed Mom and Dad a flyer.

Are you ugly?

Are you very very ugly?

Do you look like the creature from the black lagoon? (Only worse?)

Then today is your lucky day!

HENRY'S
MARVELOUS MAKEOVERS.

Only $2 for an exciting new you!!!!!!

"So, how many makeovers would you like?" said Horrid Henry. "Ten? Twenty? Maybe more 'cause you're so old and need a lot of work to fix you."

"Make over someone else," said Mom, scowling.

"Make over someone else," said Dad, scowling.

Boy, talk about ungrateful, thought Horrid Henry.

"Me first!"

"No me!"

Screams were coming from Margaret's garden. Kung-Fu Kate and Singing Soraya were about to become her latest victims. Well, not if Henry could help it.

"Step right up, get your makeovers here!" shouted Henry. "Miracle Makeovers, from an expert. Only $2 for a brand-new you."

"Leave my customers alone, copycat!"

hissed Moody Margaret, holding out her hand to snatch Kate's dollar.

Henry ignored her.

"You look boring, Kate," said Henry. "Why don't you let a *real* expert give you a makeover?"

"You?" said Kate.

"Two dollars and you'll look completely different," said Horrid Henry. "Guaranteed."

"Margaret's only charging $1," said Kate.

"My special offer today is 75 cents for

87

the first makeover," said Henry quickly. "And free beauty advice," he added.

Soraya looked up. Kate stood up from Margaret's chair.

"Such as?" scowled Margaret. "Go on, tell us."

Eeeek. What on earth *was* a beauty tip? If your face is dirty, wash it? Use a lice comb? Horrid Henry had no idea.

"Well, in your case, wear a bag over your head," said Horrid Henry. "Or a bucket."

Susan snickered.

"Ha ha, very funny," snapped Margaret. "Come on, Kate. Don't let him trick you. *I'm* the makeover expert."

"I'm going to try Henry," said Kate.

"Me too," said Soraya.

Yippee! His first customers. Henry stuck out his tongue at Margaret.

Kung-Fu Kate and Singing Soraya climbed over the wall and sat down on the bench at the picnic table. Henry opened his makeover bag and got to work.

"No peeking," said Henry. "I want you to be surprised."

Henry smeared and coated, primped and colored, slopped and glopped. This was easy!

"I'm so beautiful—hoo hoo hoo," hummed Soraya.

"Aren't you going to do my hair?" said Kung-Fu Kate.

"Of course," said Horrid Henry.

He emptied a bottle of glue on her head and scrunched it around.

"What did you put in?" said Kate.

"Secret hair potion," said Henry.

"What about *me?*" said Soraya.

"No problem," said Henry, shoveling in some red paint.

A bit of black here, a few blobs of red there, a smear of purple and…ta-da!

Henry stood back to admire his handiwork. Wow! Kung-Fu Kate looked *completely* different. So did Singing Soraya. Next time he'd charge $10. The moment people saw them everyone would want one of Henry's marvelous makeovers.

"You look amazing," said Horrid Henry. He had no idea he was such an awesome makeover artist. Customers would be lining up for his services. He'd need a bigger piggy bank.

"There, just like the Mummy,

Frankenstein, *and* a vampire," said
Henry, handing Kate a mirror.

"AAAARRRGGGGGHHH!"

screamed Kung-Fu Kate.

Soraya snatched the mirror.

"AAAARRRGGGGGHHH!"

screamed Singing Soraya.

Horrid Henry stared at them. Honestly,
there was no pleasing some people.

"NOOOOOOOOOO!"

squealed Kung-Fu Kate.

"But I thought you wanted to look
amazing," said Henry.

"Amazingly good! Not scary!" wailed
Kate.

"Has anyone seen my new lipsticks?"
said Mom. "I could have sworn I put
them in the—"

She caught sight of Soraya and Kate.

"AAAAAAARRRRRGGGGGHHHH!"

screeched Mom. "Henry! How could you be so horrid? Go to your room."

"But…but…" gasped Horrid Henry. It was so unfair. Was it his fault his stupid customers didn't know when they looked great?

Henry stomped up the stairs. Then he sighed. Maybe he did need a little more makeover practice before he opened for business.

Now, where could he find someone to practice on?

"I got an A on my spelling test," said Perfect Peter.

"I got a gold star for having the tidiest desk," said Tidy Ted.

"And I got in the Good as Gold book again," said Goody-Goody Gordon.

Henry burst into Peter's bedroom.

"I'm doing makeovers," said Horrid Henry. "Who wants to go first?"

"Ummm," said Peter.

"Ummm," said Ted.

"We're going to Sam's birthday party today," said Gordon.

"Even better," said Henry beaming. "I can make you look great for the party. Who's first?"

HORRID HENRY'S ARCH ENEMY

"Be bop a lu la!" boomed Jazzy Jim, be-bopping around the class and bouncing to the beat.

"One day, my prince will come…" warbled Singing Soraya.

"Bam bam bam bam bam!" drummed Horrid Henry, crashing his books up and down on his table top.

"Class! Settle down!" shouted Miss Battle-Axe.

"Be bop a lu la!" boomed Jazzy Jim.

"One day, my prince will come…" warbled Singing Soraya.

"Bam bam bam bam bam!" drummed Horrid Henry.

"Jim!" barked Miss Battle-Axe. "Stop yowling. Soraya! Stop singing. Henry! Stop banging or everyone will miss playtime."

"Be bop—" faltered Jim.

"...Prince will—" squeaked Soraya.

"Bam bam bam bam bam," drummed Horrid Henry. He was Mad Moon Madison, crazy drummer for the Moldy

Drumsticks, whipping the shrieking crowd into a frenzy—

"HENRY!" bellowed Miss Battle-Axe. "STOP THAT NOISE!"

What did that ungrateful fan mean, noise? What noise? This wasn't noise, this was great music, this was—Mad Moon Madison looked up from his drum kit. Whoops.

Silence.

Miss Battle-Axe glared at her class. Oh, for the good old days, when teachers could whack horrible children with rulers.

"Linda! Stop snoring. Graham! Stop drooling. Bert! Where's your chair?"

"I dunno," said Beefy Bert.

There was a new boy standing next

to Miss Battle-Axe. His brown hair was
tightly slicked back. His shoes were
polished. He carried a trumpet and
a calculator. Yuck! He looked like a
complete idiot. Horrid Henry looked
away. And then looked back. Funny,
there was something familiar about that
boy. The way he stood with his nose
in the air. The horrid little smirk on his

face. He looked like—he looked just
like—oh no, please no, it couldn't be—
Bossy Bill! Bossy Bill!!

"Class, we have a new boy," said Miss
Battle-Axe, doing her best to twist her
thin lips into a welcoming smile. "I
need someone to look after him and
show him around. Who would like to
be Bill's friend for the day?"

Everyone put up their hand. Everyone
but Horrid Henry. Uggh. Bossy Bill.
What kind of cruel joke was this?

Bossy Bill was the horrible, stuck-up son of Dad's boss. Horrid Henry hated Bill. Uggh! Yuck! Just thinking about Bill made Henry gag.

Henry had a suspicion he wasn't Bill's favorite person either. The last time they'd met, Henry had tricked Bill into photocopying his bottom. Bill had got into trouble. Big, big trouble.

Miss Battle-Axe scanned the sea of waving hands.

"Me!" shouted Moody Margaret.

"Me!" shouted Kind Kasim.

"Me!" shouted Weepy William.

"There's an empty seat next to Henry," said Miss Battle-Axe, pointing. "Henry will look after you."

NO, thought Henry.

"Waaaaaa," wailed Weepy William. "I didn't get picked."

"Go and sit down, Bill," continued

Miss Battle-Axe. "Class, silent reading from page 12."

Bossy Bill walked between the tables toward Horrid Henry.

Maybe he won't recognize me, thought Henry hopefully. After all, it was a long time ago.

Suddenly Bill stopped. His face contorted with loathing.

Oops.

He recognized me, thought Horrid Henry.

Bill marched, scowling, to the seat next to Henry and sat down. His nose wrinkled as if he smelled a stinky smell.

"You say one word about what happened at my dad's office and I'll tell my dad," hissed Bill.

"You say one word to your dad and I'll tell everyone at school you photocopied your bottom," hissed Henry.

"Then I'll tell on you!"

"I'll tell on you!"

Bill shoved Henry.

Henry shoved Bill.

"He shoved me, Miss!" shouted Bossy Bill.

"He shoved me first!" shouted Horrid Henry.

"Henry!" said Miss Battle-Axe. "I am shocked and appalled. Is this how you welcome a new boy to our class?"

It is when the boy is Bossy Bill, thought Henry grimly.

He glared at Bill.

Bill glared at Henry.

"My old school's a lot better than this dump," hissed Bossy Bill.

"So why don't you go back there?" hissed Henry. "No one's stopping you."

"Maybe I will," said Bill.

Horrid Henry's heart leaped. Was there a chance he could get Bill to leave?

"You don't want to stay here—we get four hours of homework a night," lied Henry.

"So?" said Bill. "My old school gave you five hours."

"The food's horrible."

"Big deal," said Bill.

"And Miss Battle-Axe is the meanest teacher in the world."

"What did you say, Henry?" demanded Miss Battle-Axe's ice cold dagger voice.

"I just told Bill you were the keenest teacher in the world," said Henry quickly.

"No he didn't," said Bill. "He said you were the meanest."

"Keenest," said Henry.

"Meanest," said Bill.

Miss Battle-Axe glared at Horrid Henry.

"I'm watching you, Henry. Now get back to work."

DING! DING! DING!

Hurray! Saved by the playtime bell.

Horrid Henry jumped from his seat.
Maybe he could escape Bill if he ran out
of class fast enough.

Henry pushed and shoved his way
into the hall. Free! Free at last!

"Hey!" came an unwelcome voice
beside him. A sweaty hand pulled on
his shirt.

"The teacher said you're supposed to
show me around," said Bossy Bill.

"OK, here are the bathrooms," snarled
Horrid Henry, waving his hand in
the direction of the girls' bathroom.

"And the photocopier's in the office,"
he added, pointing. "Why don't you try
it out?"

Bill scowled.

"I'm going to tell my dad that you
attacked me," said Bill. "In fact, I'm
going to tell my dad every single bad
thing you do in school. Then he'll tell
yours and you'll get into trouble. And
won't I laugh."

Henry's blood boiled. What had he
ever done to deserve Bossy Bill butting
into his life? A spy in his class. Could
school get any worse?

Aerobic Al jogged past.

"Henry photocopied his bottom at my
dad's office," said Bill loudly. "Boy, did
he get into trouble."

AAARRRGGHHH!

"That's a lie," said Horrid Henry hotly.
"Bill did, not me."

"Yeah right, Henry," said Dizzy Dave.

"Big bottom!" shrieked Moody
Margaret.

"Big, big bottom!" shrieked Sour Susan.

Bill smirked.

"Bye, big bottom," said Bill. "Don't
forget, I'm watching you," he hissed.

Henry sat down by himself on the
broken bench in the secret garden. He
had to get Bill out of his class. School
was horrible enough without someone
evil like Bill spying on him and

spreading nasty rumors. His life would be ruined. He had to get rid of Bill— fast. But how?

Maybe he could get Bill to run screaming from school and never come back. Wow, thought Horrid Henry. Wouldn't that be wonderful? Bye-bye Bossy Bill.

Or maybe he could get Bill to photocopy his bottom again. Probably not, thought Horrid Henry regretfully. Aha! He could trick Bill into dancing nude on Miss Battle-Axe's desk singing "I'm a busy bumblebee—buzz buzz buzz." That would be sure to get him expelled. The only trouble was—how?

I've got to think of something, thought Horrid Henry desperately. I've just got to.

★ ★ ★

"Henry," said Dad the next evening, "my boss tells me you've been picking on his son. Bill was very upset."

"He's picking on *me*," protested Henry.

"And that you were yelled at in class for shouting out."

"No way," lied Henry.

"And that you broke Andrew's pencil."

"That was an accident," said Henry.

"And that you called Margaret bug-face."

"I didn't," wailed Henry. "Bill's lying."

"I want you to be on your best behavior from now on," said Dad. "How do you think I feel hearing these reports about you from my boss? I've never been so embarrassed in my life."

"Who cares?" screamed Horrid Henry. "What about me?"

"Go to your room!" shouted Dad.

"FINE!" yelled Horrid Henry, slamming the door behind him as hard as he could. I'll beat you, Bill, thought Henry, if it's the last thing I do.

Horrid Henry tried teasing Bill. Horrid Henry tried pinching Bill. He tried spreading rumors about Bill. He even tried getting Bill to punch him so Bill would be suspended.

But nothing worked. Henry just got into more and more trouble.

On Monday, Dad yelled at Henry for making rude noises in class.

On Tuesday, Dad yelled at Henry for talking during story time.

On Wednesday, Dad yelled at Henry for not handing in his homework.

On Thursday, Mom and Dad yelled at Henry for chewing gum in class,

passing notes to Ralph, throwing
food, jiggling his desk, pulling
Margaret's hair, running down the
hall, and kicking a football into the
back playground. Then they banned
him from the computer for a week.
And all because of Bossy Bill.

★ ★ ★

Horrid Henry slunk into class. It was
hopeless. Bill was here to stay. Horrid
Henry would just have to grit his teeth
and bear it.

Miss Battle-Axe started explaining
electricity.

Henry looked around the classroom.

Speaking of Bill, where was he?

Maybe he has rabies, thought Horrid
Henry hopefully. Or fallen down the
toilet. Better still,
maybe he'd been
kidnapped by
aliens.

Or maybe he'd
been expelled.
Yes! Henry could
see it now. Bill on
his knees in Mrs.
Oddbod's office,

begging to stay. Mrs. Oddbod pointing
to the door:

"Out of this school, you horrible
monster! How dare you spy on Henry,
our best pupil?"

"NOOO!" Bill would wail.

"BEGONE, WRETCH!" commanded
Mrs. Oddbod. And out went Bossy Bill,
sniveling, where armed
guards were waiting
to handcuff him and
take him to prison.
That must be
what had happened.

Henry smiled.
Oh joyful day!
No more
Bossy Bill,
thought
Horrid
Henry

happily, stretching his legs under his
Bill-free table and taking a deep breath
of Bill-free air.

"Henry!" snapped Miss Battle-Axe.
"Come here."

What now?

Slowly Horrid Henry heaved himself
out of his chair and scuffed his way to
Miss Battle-Axe's desk, where she
was busy slashing at homework with a
bright red pen.

"Bill has a sore throat," said Miss Battle-Axe.

Rats, thought Horrid Henry. Where was the black plague when you needed it?

"His parents want him to have his homework assignments so he doesn't fall behind while he's sick," said Miss Battle-Axe. "If only *all* parents were so conscientious. Please give this math worksheet to your father to give to Bill's dad."

She handed Henry a piece of paper with ten multiplication sums on it and a large envelope.

"OK," said Henry dully. Not even the thought of Bill lying in bed doing sums could cheer him up. All too soon Bill would be back. He was stuck with Bill forever.

That night Horrid Henry glanced at Bill's math worksheet. Ten sums. Not enough, really, he thought. Why should Bill be bored in bed with nothing to do but watch TV, and read comics, and eat chips?

And then Horrid Henry smiled. Bill wanted homework? Perhaps Henry could help. Tee-hee, thought Horrid Henry, sitting down at the computer.

TAP.

TAP.

TAP.

HOMEWERK
Rite a storee abowt yor day. 20 pages long.

Ha ha ha, that will keep Bill busy, thought Horrid Henry. Now, what else? What else?

Aha!

Give ten reesons why watching TV is better than reading

NEW MATH
When does 2 + 2 =5 ?
When 2 is big enough.
Now explain why:
2+3=6
7-3=5

It was a lot more fun making up homework than doing it, thought Horrid Henry happily.

SPELLING:

Lern how to spel these words fer a test on Tuesday.

Terrantula

Stinkbomb

Moosli

Doovay

Screem

Intergalactik

SCEINSE

Gravity: does it work?

Drop an egg from a hight of 2 in. onto your mom or dad's hed.

Record if it breaks. Drop another egg from a hight of 4 in. onto yor carpet. Does this egg break? Try this xperiment at least 12 times all over yor house.

Now that's what I call homework, thought Horrid Henry. He printed out the worksheets, popped them in the envelope with Miss Battle-Axe's sheet of sums, sealed it, and gave it to Dad.

"Bill's homework," said Henry. "Miss Battle-Axe asked me to give it to you to give to Bill's dad."

"I'll make sure he gets it," said Dad, putting the envelope in his briefcase. "I'm glad to see you're becoming friends with Bill."

★ ★ ★

Dad looked stern.

"I've got some bad news for you, Henry," said Dad the next day.

Horrid Henry froze. What was he going to get told off about now? Oh no. Had Dad found out about what he'd done at lunchtime?

"I'm afraid Bill won't be coming back to your school," said Dad. "His parents have removed him. Something about new math and a gravity experiment that went wrong."

Horrid Henry's mouth opened. No sound came out.

"Wha—?" gasped Horrid Henry.

"Gravity experiment?" said Mom. "What gravity experiment?"

"Different science group," said Henry quickly.

"Oh," said Mom.

"Oh," said Dad.

A lovely warm feeling spread from Henry's head all the way down to his toes.

"So Bill's not coming back?"

"No," said Dad. "I'm sorry that you've lost a friend."

"I'll live," beamed Horrid Henry.

PERFECT PETER'S REVENGE

....

Perfect Peter had had enough. Why oh why did he always fall for Henry's tricks?

Every time it happened he swore Henry would never ever trick him again. And every time he fell for it. How *could* he have believed that there were fairies at the bottom of the garden? Or that there was such a thing as a Fangmangler? But the time machine was the worst. The very very worst. Everyone had teased him. Even Goody-Goody Gordon asked him if he'd seen any spaceships recently.

Well, never again. His mean, horrible brother had tricked him for the very last time.

I'll get my revenge, thought Perfect Peter, pasting the last of his animal stamps into his album. I'll make Henry sorry for being so mean to me.

But what horrid mean nasty thing could he do? Peter had never tried to take revenge on anyone.

He asked Tidy Ted.

"Mess up his room," said Ted.

But Henry's room was already a mess.

He asked Spotless Sam.

"Put a spaghetti stain on his shirt," said Sam.

But Henry's shirts were already stained.

Peter picked up a copy of his favorite magazine *Best Boy*. Maybe it would have some handy hints on the perfect revenge. He searched the table of contents:

- IS <u>YOUR</u> BEDROOM AS TIDY AS IT COULD BE?
- TEN TOP TIPS FOR PLEASING YOUR PARENTS
- HOW TO POLISH YOUR TROPHIES

- **WHY MAKING YOUR BED IS GOOD FOR YOU**
- **READERS TELL US ABOUT THEIR FAVORITE CHORES!**

Reluctantly, Peter closed *Best Boy* magazine. Somehow he didn't think he'd find the answer inside. He was on his own.

I'll tell Mom that Henry eats candy in his bedroom, thought Peter. Then Henry would get into trouble. Big big trouble.

But Henry got into trouble all the time. That wouldn't be anything special.

I know, thought Peter, I'll hide Mr. Kill. Henry would never admit it, but he couldn't sleep without Mr. Kill. But so what if Henry couldn't sleep? He'd just come and jump on Peter's head or sneak downstairs and watch scary movies.

I have to think of something really, really horrid, thought Peter. It was hard for Peter to think horrid thoughts, but Peter was determined to try.

He would call Henry a horrid name,
like Ugly Toad or Poo Poo Face. *That*
would show him.

But if I did, Henry would hit me,
thought Peter.

Wait, he could tell everyone at school
that Henry wore
diapers. Henry the
big diaper. Henry
the big smelly diaper.
Henry diaper face.
Henry poopy pants.
Peter smiled happily.
That would be the
perfect revenge.

Then he stopped
smiling. Sadly, no one at school would
believe that Henry still wore diapers.
Worse, they might think that Peter still
did! Eeeek.

I've got it, thought Peter, I'll put
a muddy twig in Henry's bed. Peter

had read a great story about a younger
brother who'd done just that to a mean
older one. That would serve Henry right.

But was a muddy twig enough revenge
for all of Henry's crimes against him?

No it was not.

I give up, thought Peter, sighing. It
was hopeless. He just couldn't think of
anything horrid enough.

Peter sat down on his beautifully made
bed and opened *Best Boy* magazine.

TELL MOM HOW MUCH YOU LOVE HER!

shrieked the headline.

And then a dreadful thought tiptoed

into his head. It was so dreadful, and so horrid, that Perfect Peter could not believe that he had thought it.

"No," he gasped. "I couldn't." That was too evil.

But...but...wasn't that exactly what he wanted? A horrid revenge on a horrid brother?

"Don't do it!" begged his angel.

"Do it!" urged his devil, thrilled to

get the chance to speak. "Go on, Peter! Henry deserves it."

YES! thought Peter. He would do it. He would have revenge!

Perfect Peter sat down at the computer. Tap tap tap.

Dear Margaret,
I love you. Will you marry me?

Peter printed out the note and carefully scrawled:

HENry

There! thought Peter proudly. That looks just like Henry's writing. He folded the note, then sneaked into the garden, climbed over the wall, and left

it on the table inside Moody Margaret's Secret Club tent.

"Of course Henry loves me," said Moody Margaret, primping. "He can't help it. Everyone loves me because I'm so lovable."

"No you're not," said Sour Susan. "You're moody. And you're mean."
  "Am not!"

"Are too!"

"Am not. You're just jealous 'cause no one would *ever* want to marry you," snapped Margaret.

"I am not jealous. Anyway, Henry likes *me* the best," said Susan, waving a folded piece of paper.

"Says who?"

"Says Henry."

Margaret snatched the paper from Susan's hand and read:

TO THE BEAUTIFUL SUSAN

Oh Susan,
No one is as pretty as you,
you always smell lovely
Just Like shampoo.
HENry

Margaret sniffed. "Just like dog poo, you mean."

"I do not," shrieked Susan.

"Is this your idea of a joke?" snorted Moody Margaret, crumpling the poem.

Sour Susan was outraged.

"No. It was waiting for me on the clubhouse table. You're just jealous because Henry didn't write *you* a poem."

"Huh," said Margaret. Well, she'd show Henry. No one made a fool of her.

Margaret snatched up a pen and scribbled a reply to Henry's note.

"Take this to Henry and report straight back," she ordered. "I'll wait here for Linda and Gurinder."

"Take it yourself," said Susan sourly. Why oh why was she friends with such a mean, moody, jealous grump?

Horrid Henry was inside the Purple Hand Fort plotting death to the Secret Club and scarfing down cookies when an enemy agent peered through the entrance.

"Guard!" shrieked Henry.

But that miserable worm toad was nowhere to be found.

Henry reminded himself to fire Peter immediately.

"Halt! Who goes there?"

"I have an important message," said the Enemy.

"Make it snappy," said Henry. "I'm busy."

Susan crept beneath the branches.

"Do you really like my shampoo, Henry?" she asked.

Henry stared at Susan. She had a sick smile on her face, as if her stomach hurt.

"Huh?" said Henry.

133

"You know, my *shampoo*," said Susan, simpering.

Had Susan finally gone crazy?

"*That's* your message?" said Horrid Henry.

"No," said Susan, scowling. She tossed a scrunched-up piece of paper at Henry and marched off.

Henry opened the note:

I wouldn't marry you if you were the last creature on earth and that includes slimy toads and rattlesnakes. So there.

Margaret

Henry choked on his cookie. Marry
Margaret?! He'd rather walk around
town carrying a Walkie-Talkie-Burpy-
Slurpy-Teasy-Weasy Doll. He'd rather
learn long division. He'd rather trade
all his computer games for a Princess
Pamper Parlor. He'd rather...he'd
rather...he'd rather marry Miss Battle-
Axe than marry Margaret!

What on earth had given Margaret the crazy, horrible, revolting idea he wanted to marry *her?*

He always knew Margaret was nuts. Now he had proof. Well well well, thought Horrid Henry gleefully. Wouldn't he tease her! Margaret would never live this down.

Henry leaped over the wall and burst into the Secret Club Tent.

"Margaret, you old pants face, I wouldn't marry you if—"

"Henry loves Margaret! Henry loves Margaret!" chanted Gorgeous Gurinder.

"Henry loves Margaret! Henry loves Margaret!" chanted Lazy Linda, making horrible kissing sounds.

Henry tried to speak. He opened his mouth. Then he closed it.

"No I don't," gasped Horrid Henry.

"Oh yeah?" said Gurinder.

"Yeah," said Henry.

"Then why'd you send her a note saying you did?"

"I didn't!" howled Henry.

"And you sent Susan a poem!" said Linda.

"I DID NOT!" howled Henry even louder. What on earth was going on? He took a step backward.

The Secret Club members advanced on him, shrieking, "Henry loves Margaret, Henry loves Margaret."

Time, thought Horrid Henry, to make a strategic retreat. He dashed back to his fort, the terrible words "Henry loves Margaret" burning his ears.

"PETER!" bellowed Horrid Henry. "Come here this minute!"

Perfect Peter crept out of the house to the fort. Henry had found out about the note and the poem. He was dead.

Good-bye, cruel world, thought Peter.

"Did you see anyone going into the Secret Club carrying a note?" demanded Henry, glaring.

Perfect Peter's heart began to beat again.

"No," said Peter. That wasn't a lie because he hadn't seen himself.

"I want you to stand guard by the wall, and report anyone suspicious to me at once," said Henry.

"Why?" said Peter innocently.

"None of your business, worm," snapped Henry. "Just do as you're told."

"Yes, Lord High Excellent Majesty of the Purple Hand," said Perfect Peter. What a lucky escape!

Henry sat on his Purple Hand throne and thought. Who was this foul fiend? Who was this evil genius? Who was spreading these nasty rumors? He had to find out, then strike back hard before the snake struck again.

But who'd want to be his enemy? He was such a nice, kind, friendly boy.

True, Rude Ralph wasn't very happy when Henry called him Ralphie Walfie.

Tough Toby wasn't too pleased when Henry depantsed him during playtime.

And for some reason, Brainy Brian didn't see the joke when Henry scribbled all over his book report.

Vain Violet said she'd pay Henry back for pulling her pigtails.

And just the other day Fiery Fiona
said Henry would be sorry he'd laughed
during her speech in the assembly.

Even Kind Kasim warned Henry to
stop being so horrid or he'd teach him a
lesson he wouldn't forget.

But maybe Margaret was behind the
whole plot. He had stinkbombed her
Secret Club, after all.

Hmmm. The list of suspects was rather
long.

It had to be Ralph. Ralph loved
playing practical jokes.

Well, it's not funny, Ralph, thought
Horrid Henry. Let's see how *you*
like it. Perhaps a little poem to Miss
Battle-Axe...

Horrid Henry grabbed a piece of
paper and began to scribble:

Oh Boudicca dear,
Whenever you're near,
I just want to cheer,
Oh big old teacher
Your carrot nose is your best feature
You are so sweet
I would like to kiss your feet
What a treat
Even though they smell of meat
Dear Miss Battle-Axe
Clear out your earwax
So you can hear me say...
No need to frown
But your pants are falling down!

Ha ha ha ha ha,
thought Henry.
He'd sign the
poem "Ralph,"
get to school early,
and pin the poem
on the door of the girls' bathroom.

Ralph would get into big big trouble.

But wait.

What if Ralph *wasn't* responsible?

Could it be Toby after all? Or Margaret?

There was only one thing to do.
Henry copied his poem seven times,
signing each copy with a different name.
He would post them all over school
tomorrow. One of them was sure to
be guilty.

Henry sneaked into school, then quickly
pinned up his poems on every bulletin
board. That done, he swaggered onto the

playground. Revenge is sweet, thought Horrid Henry.

There was a crowd gathered outside the boys' bathroom.

"What's going on?" shrieked Horrid Henry, pushing and shoving his way through the crowd.

"Henry loves Margaret," chanted Tough Toby.

"Henry loves Margaret," chanted Rude Ralph.

Uh oh.

Henry glanced at the bathroom door. There was a note taped on it.

Dear Margaret,
I love you. Will you marry me?
HENry

Henry's blood froze. He ripped the note off the door.

"Margaret wrote it to herself," blustered Horrid Henry.

"Didn't!" said Margaret.

"Did!" said Henry.

"Besides, you love *me!*" shrieked Susan.

"No I don't!" shrieked Henry.

"That's 'cause you love me!" said Margaret.

"I hate you!" shouted Henry.

"I hate you more!" said Margaret.

"I hate *you* more," said Henry.

"You started it," said Margaret.

"Didn't."

"Did! You asked me to marry you."

"NO WAY!" shrieked Henry.

"And you sent me a poem!" said Susan.

"No I didn't!" howled Henry.

"Well, if you didn't then who did?" said Margaret.

Silence.

"Henry," came a little voice, "can we play pirates after school today?"

Horrid Henry thought an incredible thought.

Moody Margaret thought an incredible thought.

Sour Susan thought an incredible thought.

Three pairs of eyes stared at Perfect Peter.

"Wha...what?" said Peter.

Uh oh.

"HELP!" shrieked Perfect Peter. He turned and ran.

"AAAARRRRGHHHHHH!" shrieked Horrid Henry, chasing after him. "You're dead meat, worm!"

Miss Battle-Axe marched onto the playground. She was clutching a sheaf of papers in her hand.

"Margaret! Brian! Ralph! Toby! Violet! Kasim! Fiona! What is the meaning of these poems? Straight to the principal's office— now!" Perfect Peter crashed into her.

Smash!

Miss Battle-Axe toppled backward into the garbage.

"And you too, Peter," gasped Miss Battle-Axe.

"Waaaaaaa!" wailed Perfect Peter. From now on, he'd definitely be sticking to good deeds. Whoever said revenge was sweet didn't have a horrid brother like Henry.

HORRID HENRY'S PERFECT DAY

Henry was horrid.

Everyone said so, even his mother. Henry threw food, Henry grabbed, Henry pushed and shoved and pinched. Even his teddy bear, Mr. Kill, avoided him when possible.

His parents despaired.

"What are we going to do about that horrid boy?" sighed Mom.

"How did two people as nice as us have such a horrid child?" sighed Dad.

When Horrid Henry's parents took Henry to school they walked behind him and pretended he was not theirs.

Children pointed at Henry and whispered to their parents, "That's Horrid Henry."

"He's the boy who threw my jacket in the mud."

"He's the boy who squashed Billy's beetle."

"He's the boy who…" Fill in whatever terrible deed you like. Horrid Henry was sure to have done it.

Horrid Henry had
a younger brother.
His name was
Perfect Peter.

Perfect Peter
always said "Please"
and "Thank you."
Perfect Peter loved
vegetables.

Perfect Peter
always used a hankie
and never, ever
picked his nose.

"Why can't you
be perfect like
Peter?" said Henry's
mom every day.

As usual, Henry pretended not to hear. He continued melting Peter's crayons on the radiator.

But Horrid Henry started to think.

"What if *I* were perfect?" thought Henry. "I wonder what would happen."

When Henry woke the next morning, he did not wake Peter by pouring water on Peter's head.

Peter did not scream.

This meant Henry's parents overslept and Henry and Peter were late for Cub Scouts.

Henry was very happy.

Peter was very sad to be late for Cub Scouts.

But because he was perfect, Peter did not whine or complain.

On the way to Cub Scouts Henry did not squabble with Peter over who sat in front. He did not pinch Peter and he did not shove Peter.

Back home, when Perfect Peter built a castle, Henry did not knock it down. Instead, Henry sat on the sofa and read a book.

Mom and Dad ran into the room.

"It's awfully quiet in here," said Mom. "Are you being horrid, Henry?"

"No," said Henry.

"Peter, is Henry knocking your castle down?"

Peter longed to say "yes." But that would be a lie.

"No," said Peter.

He wondered why Henry was behaving so strangely.

"What are you doing, Henry?" said Dad.

"Reading a wonderful story about some super mice," said Henry.

Dad had never seen Henry read a book before. He checked to see if a comic was hidden inside.

There was no comic. Henry was actually reading a book.

"Hmmmm," said Dad.

★ ★ ★

It was almost time for dinner. Henry was hungry and went into the kitchen where Dad was cooking.

But instead of shouting, "I'm starving! Where's my food?" Henry said, "Dad, you look tired. Can I help get supper ready?"

"Don't be horrid, Henry," said Dad, pouring peas into boiling water. Then he stopped.

"What did you say, Henry?" asked Dad.

"Can *I* help, Dad?" said Perfect Peter.

"I asked if you needed any help," said Henry.

"I asked first," said Peter.

"Henry will just make a mess," said Dad. "Peter, would you peel the carrots while I sit down for a moment?"

157

"Of course," said
Perfect Peter.

Peter washed his
spotless hands.

Peter put on his
spotless apron.

Peter rolled up his
spotless sleeves.

Peter waited for
Henry to snatch the
peeler.

But Henry set the table instead.

Mom came into the kitchen.

"Smells good," she said. "Thank you, darling Peter, for setting the table. What a good boy you are."

Peter did not say anything.

"I set the table, Mom," said Henry.

Mom stared at him.

"You?" said Mom.

"Me," said Henry.

"Why?" said Mom.

Henry smiled.

"To be helpful," he said.

"You've done something horrid, haven't you, Henry?" said Dad.

"No," said Henry. He tried to look sweet.

"I'll set the table tomorrow," said Perfect Peter.

"Thank you, angel," said Mom.

"Dinner is ready," said Dad.

The family sat down at the table.

Dinner was spaghetti and meatballs with peas and carrots.

Henry ate his dinner with his knife and fork and spoon.

He did not throw peas at Peter and he did not slurp.

He did not chew with his mouth open and he did not slouch.

"Sit properly, Henry," said Dad.

"I am sitting properly," said Henry.

Dad looked up from his plate. He looked surprised.

"So you are," he said.

Perfect Peter could not eat. Why wasn't Henry throwing peas at him?

Peter's hand reached slowly for a pea.

When no one was looking, he
flicked the pea at Henry.

"Ouch," said Henry.

"Don't be horrid, Henry," said
Mom.

Henry reached for a fistful of peas.
Then Henry remembered he was
being perfect and stopped.

Peter smiled and waited. But no
peas bopped him on the head.

Perfect Peter did not understand.
Where was the foot that always
kicked him under the table?

Slowly, Peter stretched out his foot and kicked Henry.

"OUCH," said Henry.

"Don't be horrid, Henry," said Dad.

"But I…" said Henry, then stopped.

Henry's foot wanted to kick Perfect Peter around the block. Then Henry remembered he was being perfect and continued to eat.

"You're very quiet tonight, Henry," said Dad.

"The better to enjoy my lovely dinner," said Henry.

"Henry, where are your peas and carrots?" asked Mom.

"I ate them," said Henry. "They were delicious."

Mom looked on the floor. She looked under Henry's chair. She looked under his plate.

"You ate your peas and carrots?"
said Mom slowly. She felt Henry's
forehead.

"Are you feeling all right, Henry?"

"Yeah," said Horrid Henry. "I'm
fine, thank you for asking," he added
quickly.

Mom and Dad looked at each other. What was going on?

Then they looked at Henry.

"Henry, come here and let me give you a big kiss," said Mom. "You are a wonderful boy. Would you like a piece of fudge cake?"

Peter interrupted.

"No cake for me, thank you," said Peter. "I would rather have more vegetables."

Henry let himself be kissed. Oh my, it was hard work being perfect.

He smiled sweetly at Peter.

"I would love some cake, thank you," said Henry.

Perfect Peter could stand it no
longer. He picked up his plate and
aimed at Henry.

Then Peter threw
the spaghetti.

Henry ducked.

SPLAT!

Spaghetti landed
on Mom's head.

Tomato sauce
trickled down her
neck and down her
new yellow fuzzy
sweater.

"PETER!!!!" yelled Mom and Dad.

"YOU HORRID BOY!" yelled Mom.

"GO TO YOUR ROOM!!" yelled Dad.

Perfect Peter burst into tears and ran to his room.

Mom wiped spaghetti off her face. She looked very funny.

Henry tried not to laugh. He squeezed his lips together tightly.

But it was no use. I am sorry to say that he could not stop a laugh escaping.

"It's not funny!" shouted Dad.

"Go to your room!" shouted Mom.

But Henry didn't care.

Who would have thought being perfect would be such fun?

HORRID HENRY'S WEDDING

....

"I'm not wearing these horrible clothes and that's that!"

Horrid Henry glared at the mirror. A stranger smothered in a lilac ruffled shirt, green satin knickerbockers, tights, pink cummerbund tied in a floppy bow, and pointy white satin shoes with gold buckles glared back at him.

Henry had never seen anyone looking so silly in his life.

"Aha ha ha ha ha!" shrieked Horrid Henry, pointing at the mirror.

Then Henry peered more closely. The ridiculous looking boy was him.

Perfect Peter stood next to Horrid Henry. He too was smothered in a lilac ruffled shirt, green satin knickerbockers, tights, pink cummerbund, and pointy white shoes with gold buckles. But, unlike Henry, Peter was smiling.

"Aren't they adorable!" squealed Prissy Polly. "That's how my children are always going to dress."

Prissy Polly was Horrid Henry's horrible older cousin. Prissy Polly was always squeaking and squealing:

"Eeek, it's a speck of dust."

"Eeek, it's a puddle."

"Eeek, my hair is a mess."

But when Prissy Polly announced she was getting married to Pimply Paul and wanted Henry and Peter to be ring bearers, Mom said yes before Henry could stop her.

"What's a ring bearer?" asked Henry suspiciously.

"A ring bearer carries the wedding rings down the aisle on a satin cushion," said Mom.

"And throws confetti afterward," said Dad.

Henry liked the idea of throwing confetti. But carrying rings on a cushion? No thanks.

"I don't want to be a ring bearer," said Henry.

"I do, I do," said Peter.

"You're going to be a ring bearer, and that's that," said Mom.

"And you'll behave yourself," said Dad. "It's very kind of cousin Polly to ask you."

Henry scowled.

"Who'd want to be married to *her?*" said Henry. "I wouldn't if you paid me a million dollars."

But for some reason the groom, Pimply Paul, did want to marry Prissy Polly. And, as far as Henry knew, he had not been paid one million dollars.

Pimply Paul was also trying on his wedding clothes. He looked ridiculous in a black top hat, lilac shirt, and a black jacket covered in gold swirls.

"I won't wear these silly clothes," said Henry.

"Oh be quiet, you little brat," snapped Pimply Paul.

Horrid Henry glared at him.

"I won't," said Henry. "And that's final."

"Henry, stop being horrid," said Mom. She looked extremely silly in a big floppy hat dripping with flowers.

Suddenly Henry grabbed at the lace ruffles around his throat.

"I'm choking," he gasped. "I can't breathe."

Then Henry fell to the floor and rolled around.

"Uggggghhhhhhh," moaned Henry. "I'm dying."

"Get up this minute, Henry!" said Dad.

"Eeek, there's dirt on the floor!" shrieked Polly.

"Can't you control that child?" hissed Pimply Paul.

"I DON'T WANT TO BE A RING
BEARER!" howled Horrid Henry.

"Thank you so much for asking me
to be a ring bearer, Polly," shouted
Perfect Peter, trying to be heard over
Henry's screams.

"You're welcome," shouted Polly.

"Stop that, Henry!" ordered Mom.
"I've never been so ashamed in my life."

"I hate children," muttered Pimply
Paul under his breath.

Horrid Henry stopped. Unfortunately,
his ring bearer clothes looked as fresh
and crisp as ever.

All right, thought Horrid Henry. You
want me at this wedding? You've got me.

Prissy Polly's wedding day arrived.
Henry was delighted to see rain pouring
down. How mad Polly would be.

Perfect Peter was already dressed.

"Isn't this going to be fun, Henry?" said Peter.

"No!" said Henry, sitting on the floor. "And I'm not going."

Mom and Dad stuffed Henry into his ring bearer clothes. It was hard, heavy work.

Finally everyone was in the car.

"We're going to be late!" shrieked Mom.

"We're going to be late!" shrieked Dad.

"We're going to be late!" shrieked Peter.

"Good!" muttered Henry.

Mom, Dad, Henry, and Peter arrived at the church. Boom! There was a clap of thunder. Rain poured down. All the other guests were already inside.

"Watch out for the puddle, boys," said Mom, as she leaped out of the car. She opened her umbrella.

Dad jumped over the puddle.

Peter jumped over the puddle.

Henry jumped over the puddle, and tripped.

SPLASH!

"Oopsy," said Henry.

His ruffles were torn, his knickerbockers were filthy, and his satin shoes were soaked.

Mom, Dad, and Peter were covered in muddy water.

Perfect Peter burst into tears.

"You've ruined my ring bearer clothes," sobbed Peter.

Mom wiped as much dirt as she could off Henry and Peter.

"It was an accident, Mom, really," said Henry.

"Hurry up, you're late!" shouted Pimply Paul.

Mom and Dad dashed into the church. Henry and Peter stayed outside, waiting to make their entrance.

Pimply Paul and his best man, Cross Colin, stared at Henry and Peter.

"You look like a mess," said Paul.

"It was an accident," said Henry.

Peter sniveled.

"Now be careful with the wedding rings," said Cross Colin. He handed

Henry and Peter a satin cushion each, with a gold ring on top.

A great quivering clump of lace and taffeta and bows and flowers approached. Henry guessed Prissy Polly must be lurking somewhere underneath.

"Eeek," squeaked the clump. "Why did it have to rain on my wedding?"

"Eeek," squeaked the clump again. "You're filthy."

Perfect Peter began to sob. The satin cushion trembled in his hand. The ring balanced precariously near the edge.

Cross Colin snatched Peter's cushion.

"You can't carry a ring with your hand shaking like that," snapped Colin. "You'd better carry them both, Henry."

"Come *on*," hissed Pimply Paul. "We're late!"

Cross Colin and Pimply Paul dashed into the church.

The music started. Henry pranced down the aisle after Polly. Everyone stood up.

Henry beamed and bowed and waved. He was King Henry the Horrible, smiling graciously at his cheering subjects before he chopped off their heads.

As he danced along, he stepped on Polly's long, trailing dress. Riiiiip.

"Eeeeek!" squeaked Prissy Polly.

Part of Polly's train lay beneath Henry's muddy satin shoe.

That dress was too long anyway, thought Henry. He kicked the fabric out of the way and stomped down the aisle.

The bride, groom, best man, and ring bearers assembled in front of the minister.

Henry stood…and stood…and stood. The minister droned on…and on…

and on. Henry's arm holding up the
cushion began to ache.

This is boring, thought Henry, jiggling
the rings on the cushion.

Boing! Boing! Boing!

Oooh, thought Henry. I'm good at
ring tossing.

The rings bounced.

The minister droned.

Henry was a famous pancake chef,
tossing the pancakes higher and higher
and higher...

Clink clunk.

The rings rolled down the aisle and
vanished down a small grate.

Oops, thought Henry.

"May I have the rings, please?" said the
minister.

Everyone looked at Henry.

"He's got them," said Henry
desperately, pointing at Peter.

"I do not," sobbed Peter.

Henry reached into his pocket. He found two pieces of old chewing gum, some gravel, and his lucky pirate ring.

"Here, use this," he said.

At last, Pimply Paul and Prissy Polly were married.

Cross Colin handed Henry and Peter a basket of pink and yellow rose petals each.

"Throw the petals in front of the bride and groom as they walk back down the aisle," whispered Colin.

"I will," said Peter. He scattered the petals before Pimply Paul and Prissy Polly.

"So will I," said Henry. He hurled a handful of petals in Pimply Paul's face.

"Watch it, you little brat," snarled Paul.

"Windy, isn't it?" said Henry. He hurled another handful of petals at Polly.

"Eeek," squeaked Prissy Polly.

"Everyone outside for the photographs," said the photographer.

Horrid Henry loved having his picture taken. He dashed out.

"Pictures of the bride and groom first,"
said the photographer.

Henry jumped in front.

Click.

Henry peeked from the side.

Click.

Henry stuck out his tongue.

Click.

Henry made horrible rude faces.

Click.

"This way to the reception!" said Cross Colin.

★ ★ ★

The wedding party was held in a nearby
hotel.

The adults did nothing but talk and
eat, talk and drink, talk and eat.

Perfect Peter sat at the table and ate his
lunch.

Horrid Henry sat under the table and
poked people's legs. He crawled around
and squashed some toes. Then Henry got
bored and drifted into the next room.

There was the wedding cake, standing
alone, on a little table. It was the most
beautiful, delicious looking cake Henry
had ever seen. It had three layers and
was covered in luscious white icing and
yummy iced flowers and bells and leaves.

Henry's mouth watered.

I'll just taste a teeny weeny bit of petal,
thought Henry. No harm in that.

He broke off a morsel and popped it in
his mouth.

Mmmmm boy! That icing tasted great.

Perhaps just one more bite, thought Henry. If I take it from the back, no one will notice.

Henry carefully selected an icing rose from the bottom tier and stuffed it in his mouth. Wow.

Henry stood back from the cake. It looked a little uneven now, with that rose missing from the bottom.

I'll just even it up, thought Henry. It was the work of a moment to break off a rose from the middle tier and another from the top.

Then a strange thing happened.

"Eat me," whispered the cake. "Go on."

Who was Henry to ignore such a request?

He picked out a few crumbs from the back.

Delicious, thought Henry. Then he took a few more. And a few more. Then he dug out a nice big chunk.

"What do you think you're doing?" shouted Pimply Paul.

Henry ran around the cake table. Paul ran after him.

Around and around and around the cake they ran.

"Just wait till I get my hands on you!" snarled Pimply Paul.

Henry dashed under the table.

Pimply Paul lunged for him and missed.

SPLAT.

Pimply Paul fell headfirst onto the cake.

Henry slipped away.

Prissy Polly ran into the room.

"Eeek," she shrieked.

"Wasn't that a lovely wedding?" sighed Mom on the way home. "Funny they didn't have a cake, though."

"Oh yes," said Dad.

"Oh yes," said Peter.

"OH YES!" said Henry. "I'll be glad to be a ring bearer anytime."

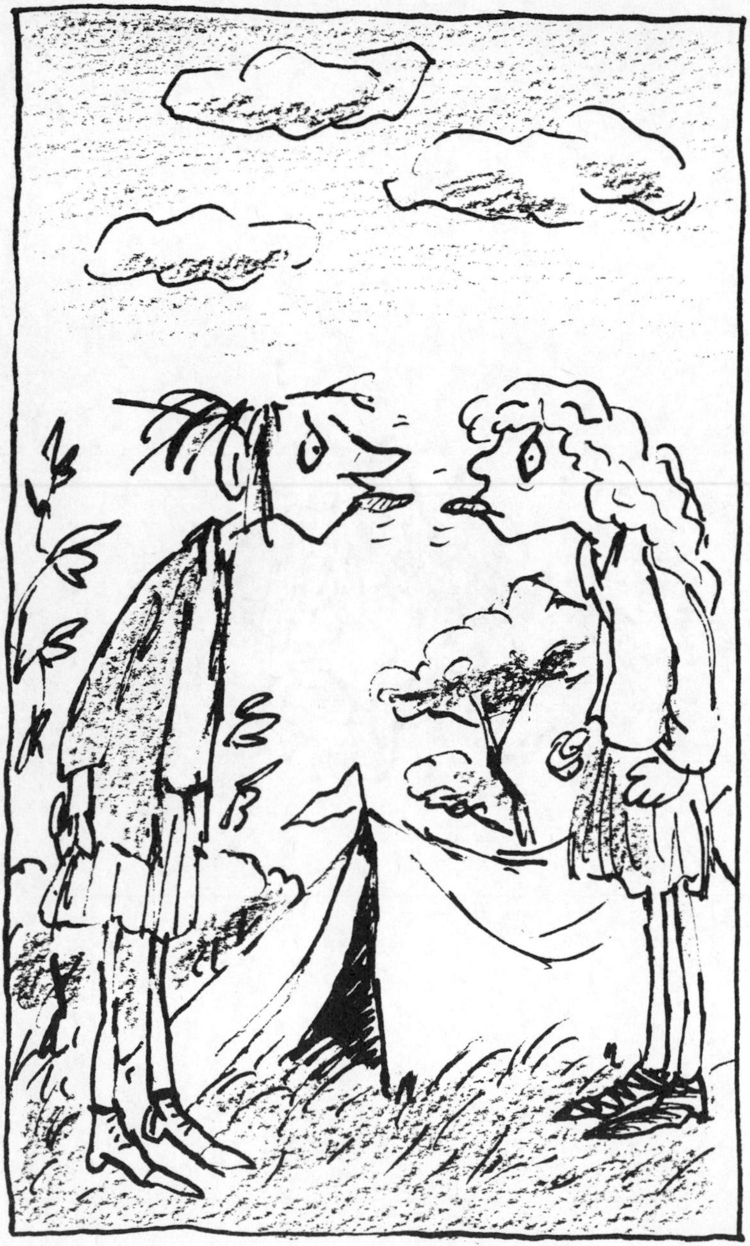

HORRID HENRY'S STINKBOMB

....

"I hate you, Margaret!" shrieked Sour Susan. She stumbled out of the Secret Club tent.

"I hate you too!" shrieked Moody Margaret.

Sour Susan stuck out her tongue.

Moody Margaret stuck out hers back.

"I quit!" yelled Susan.

"You can't quit. You're fired!" yelled Margaret.

"You can't fire me. I quit!" said Susan.

"I fired you first," said Margaret. "And I'm changing the password!"

"Go ahead. See if I care. I don't want

to be in the Secret Club any more!"
said Susan sourly.

"Good! Because *we* don't want you."

Moody Margaret flounced back
inside the Secret Club tent. Sour Susan
stalked off.

Free at last! Susan was sick and
tired of her ex-best friend Bossyboots
Margaret. Blaming *her* for the disastrous
raid on the Purple Hand Fort when it
was all Margaret's fault was bad enough.
But then to ask stupid Linda to join the
Secret Club without even telling her!
Susan hated Linda even more than she
hated Margaret. Linda hadn't invited
Susan to her sleepover party. And she
was a copycat. But Margaret didn't
care. Today she'd made Linda chief spy.
Well, Susan had had enough. Margaret
had been mean to her once too often.

Susan heard roars of laughter from
inside the club tent. So they were

laughing, were they? Laughing at her, no doubt? Well, she'd show them. She knew all about Margaret's Top Secret Plans. And she knew someone who would be very interested in that information.

"Halt! Password!"

"Smelly toads," said Perfect Peter. He waited outside Henry's Purple Hand Fort.

"Wrong," said Horrid Henry.

"What's the new one then?" said Perfect Peter.

"I'm not telling *you*," said Henry. "You're fired, remember?"

Perfect Peter did remember. He had hoped Henry had forgotten.

"Can't I join again, Henry?" asked Peter.

"No way!" said Horrid Henry.

"Please?" said Perfect Peter.

"No," said Horrid Henry. "Ralph's taken over your duties."

Rude Ralph poked his head through the branches of Henry's lair.

"No babies allowed," said Rude Ralph.

"We don't want you here, Peter," said Horrid Henry. "Get lost."

Perfect Peter burst into tears.

"Crybaby!" jeered Horrid Henry.

"Crybaby!" jeered Rude Ralph.

That did it.

"Mom!" wailed Perfect Peter. He ran toward the house. "Henry won't let me play and he called me a crybaby!"

"Stop being horrid, Henry!" shouted Mom.

Peter waited.

Mom didn't say anything else.

Perfect Peter started to wail louder.

"Mooom! Henry's being mean to me!"

"Leave Peter alone, Henry!" shouted Mom. She came out of the house. Her hands were covered in dough. "Henry, if you don't stop—"

Mom looked around.

"Where's Henry?"

"In his fort," sniveled Peter.

"I thought you said he was being mean to you," said Mom.

"He was!" wailed Peter.

"Just keep away from him," said Mom. She went back into the house.

Perfect Peter was outraged. Was that it? Why hadn't she punished Henry? Henry had been so horrid he deserved to go to prison for a year. Two years. And just get a crust of bread a week. And brussels sprouts. Ha! That would serve Henry right.

195

But until Henry went to prison, how could Peter pay him back?

And then Peter knew exactly what he could do.

He checked carefully to see that no one was watching. Then he sneaked over the garden wall and headed for the Secret Club Tent.

"He isn't!" said Margaret.

"She wouldn't," said Henry.

"He's planning to swap our lemonade for a Dungeon Drink?" said Margaret.

"Yes," said Peter.

"She's planning to stinkbomb the Purple Hand Fort?" said Henry.

"Yes," said Susan.

"How dare she?" said Henry.

"How dare he?" said Margaret. "I'll easily put a stop to that. Linda!" she barked. "Hide the lemonade!"

Linda yawned.

"Hide it yourself," she said. "I'm tired."

Margaret glared at her, then hid the jug under a box.

"Ha ha! Won't Henry be shocked

when he sneaks over and there are no drinks to spike!" gloated Margaret. "Peter, you're a hero. I award you the Triple Star, the highest honor the Secret Club can bestow."

"Ooh, thanks!" said Peter. It was nice being appreciated for a change.

"So from now on," said Moody Margaret, "you're working for me."

"Okay," said the traitor.

Horrid Henry rubbed his hands. This was fantastic! At last, he had a spy in the enemy's camp! He'd easily defend himself against that stupid stinkbomb. Margaret would only let it off when he was *in* the fort. His sentry would be on the lookout armed with a goo-shooter. When Margaret tried to sneak in with her stinkbomb—ker-pow!

"Hang on a sec," said Horrid Henry, "why should I trust you?"

"Because Margaret is mean and horrible and I hate her," said Susan.

"So from now on," said Horrid Henry, "you're working for me."

Susan wasn't sure she liked the sound of that. Then she remembered Margaret's mean cackle.

"Okay," said the traitor.

Peter sneaked back into his garden and collided with someone.

"Ouch!" said Peter.

"Watch where you're going!" snapped Susan.

They glared at each other suspiciously.

"What were you doing at Margaret's?" said Susan.

"Nothing," said Peter. "What were you doing at my house?"

"Nothing," said Susan.

Peter walked toward Henry's fort, whistling.

Susan walked toward Margaret's tent, whistling.

Well, if Susan was spying on Henry for Margaret, Peter certainly wasn't going to warn him. Serve Henry right.

Well, if Peter was spying on Margaret for Henry, Susan certainly wasn't going to warn her. Serve Margaret right.

Dungeon Drinks, eh?

Margaret liked that idea much better than her stinkbomb plot.

"I've changed my mind about the stinkbomb," said Margaret. "I'm going to swap his drinks for Dungeon Drink stinkers instead."

"Good idea," said Lazy Linda. "Less work."

Stinkbomb, eh?

Henry liked that much better than his Dungeon Drink plot. Why hadn't he thought of that himself?

"I've changed my mind about the Dungeon Drinks," said Henry. "I'm going to stinkbomb her instead."

"Yeah," said Rude Ralph. "When?"

"Now," said Horrid Henry. "Come on, let's go to my room."

Horrid Henry opened his Stinky Stinkbomb kit. He'd bought it with Grandma. Mom would *never* have let him buy it. But because Grandma had given him the money Mom couldn't do anything about it. Ha ha ha.

Now, which stink would he pick?
He looked at the test tubes filled with
powder and read the gruesome labels.

Bad breath. Dog poo. Rotten eggs.
Smelly socks. Dead fish. Sewer stench.

"I'd go for dead fish," said Ralph.
"That's the worst."

Henry considered.

"How about we mix dead fish *and*
rotten eggs?"

"Yeah," said Rude Ralph.

Slowly, carefully, Horrid Henry
measured out a teaspoon of dead fish
powder, and a teaspoon of rotten egg
powder, into the special pouch.

Slowly, carefully, Rude Ralph poured out 150 milliliters of secret stinkbomb liquid into the bottle and capped it tightly. All they had to do was to add

the powder to the bottle outside the Secret Club—and run!

"Ready?" said Horrid Henry.

"Ready," said Rude Ralph.

"Whatever you do," said Horrid Henry, "don't spill it."

"So you've come crawling back," said Moody Margaret. "I knew you would."

"No," said Sour Susan. "I just happened to be passing."

She looked around the Secret Club Tent.

"Where's Linda?"

Margaret scowled. "Gone."

"Gone for today, or gone forever?" said Susan.

"Forever," said Margaret savagely. "I don't ever want to see that lazy lump again."

Margaret and Susan looked at each other.

Susan tapped her foot.

Margaret hummed.

"Well?" said Margaret.

"Well what?" said Susan.

"Are you rejoining the Secret Club as Chief Spy or aren't you?"

"I might," said Susan. "And I might not."

"Suit yourself," said Margaret. "I'll call Gurinder and ask her to join instead."

"Okay," said Susan quickly. "I'll join."

Should she mention her visit to Henry?
Better not. After all, what Margaret
didn't know wouldn't hurt her.

"Now, about my stinkbomb plot,"
began Margaret. "I decided—"

Something shattered on the ground
inside the tent. A ghastly, gruesome,
grisly stinky stench filled the air.

"AAAAARGGGGG!" screamed
Margaret, gagging. "It's a—
STINKBOMB!"

"HELP!" shrieked Sour Susan.
"STINKBOMB! Help! Help!"

Victory! Horrid Henry and Rude Ralph ran back to the Purple Hand Fort and rolled around the floor, laughing and shrieking.

What a triumph!

Margaret and Susan screaming! Margaret's mom screaming! Margaret's dad screaming! And the stink! Wow! Horrid Henry had never smelled anything so awful in his life.

This called for a celebration.

Horrid Henry offered Ralph a fistful of candy and poured out two glasses of Fizzywizz drinks.

"Cheers!" said Henry.

"Cheers!" said Ralph.

They drank.

"AAAAAARRGGGGGG!" choked Rude Ralph.

"Blecccccch!" yelped Horrid Henry, gagging and spitting. "We've been—" cough!— "Dungeon-Drinked!"

And then Horrid Henry heard a horrible sound. Moody Margaret and Sour Susan were outside the Purple Hand Fort. Chanting a victory chant: "NAH NAH NE NAH NAH!"

HORRiD HENRY'S SLEEPOVER

Horrid Henry loved sleepovers.
Midnight feasts! Pillow fights! Screaming
and shouting! Rampaging till dawn!

The time he ate all the ice cream at
Greedy Graham's and left the freezer
door open! The time he jumped on
all the beds at Dizzy Dave's and broke
them all. And that time at Rude Ralph's
when he—well, hmmm, perhaps better
not mention that.

There was just one problem. No one
would ever have Horrid Henry at their
house for a sleepover more than once.
Whenever Henry went to sleep at a
friend's house, Mom and Dad were sure

to get a call at three
a.m. from a demented
parent screaming
at them to pick up
Henry immediately.

Horrid Henry
couldn't understand it.
Parents were so fussy.
Even the parents of
great kids like Rude
Ralph and Greedy Graham. Who cares
about a little noise? Or a broken bed?
Big deal, thought Horrid Henry.

It was no fun having friends sleep over
at *his* house. There was no
rampaging and feasting at Henry's. It
was lights out as usual at nine o'clock,
no talking, no feasting, no fun.

So when New Nick, who had just
joined Henry's class, invited Henry to
stay the night, Horrid Henry couldn't
believe his luck. New beds to bounce on.

New cookie jars to raid. New places to rampage. Bliss!

Henry packed his sleepover bag as fast as he could.

Mom came in. She looked grumpy.

"Got your pajamas?" she asked.

Henry never needed pajamas at sleepovers because he never went to bed.

"Got them," said Henry. Just not *with* him, he thought.

"Don't forget your toothbrush," said Mom.

"I won't," said Horrid Henry. He never *forgot* his toothbrush—he just chose not to bring it.

Dad came in. He looked even grumpier.

"Don't forget your comb," said Dad.

Horrid Henry looked at his bulging backpack stuffed with toys and comics. Sadly, there was no room for a comb.

"I won't," lied Henry.

"I'm warning you, Henry," said Mom. "I want you to be on best behavior tonight."

"Of course," said Horrid Henry.

"I don't want any phone calls at three a.m. from Nick's parents," said Dad. "If I do, this will be your last sleepover ever. I mean it."

Nag nag nag.

"All right," said Horrid Henry.

Ding Dong.

WOOF WOOF WOOF WOOF WOOF!

A woman opened the door. She was wearing a Viking helmet on her head and long flowing robes. Behind her stood a man in a velvet cloak holding back five enormous, snarling black dogs.

"TRA LA LA BOOM-DY AY," boomed a dreadful, earsplitting voice.

"Bravo, Bravo!" shouted a chorus from the sitting room.

GRRRRRRR! growled the dogs.

Horrid Henry hesitated. Did he have the right house? Was New Nick an alien?

"Oh don't mind us, dear, it's our opera club's karaoke night," trilled the Viking helmet.

"Nick!" bellowed the Cloak. "Your friend is here."

Nick appeared. Henry was glad to see he was not wearing a Viking helmet or a velvet cloak.

"Hi Henry," said New Nick.

"Hi Nick," said Horrid Henry.

A little girl toddled over, sucking her thumb.

"Henry, this is my sister, Lily," said Nick.

Lily gazed at Horrid Henry.

"I love you, Henwy," said Lisping Lily. "Will you marry with me?"

"NO!" said Horrid Henry. Uggh.
What a revolting thought.

"Go away, Lily," said Nick.

Lily did not move.

"Come on, Nick, let's get out of
here," said Henry. No toddler was
going to spoil *his* fun. Now, what
would he do first, raid the kitchen or
bounce on the beds?

"Let's raid the kitchen," said Henry.

"Great," said Nick.

"Got any good candy?" asked Henry.

"Tons!" said New Nick.

Yeah! thought Horrid Henry. His sleepover fun was beginning!

They sneaked into the kitchen. The floor was covered with dog blankets, overturned food bowls, clumps of dog hair, and gnawed dog bones. There were a few suspicious looking puddles. Henry hoped they were water.

"Here are the cookies," said Nick.

Henry looked. Were those dog hairs all over the jar?

"Uh, no thanks," said Henry. "How about some candy?"

"Sure," said Nick. "Help yourself."

He handed Henry a bar of chocolate. Yummy! Henry was about to take a big

bite when he stopped. Were those—
teeth marks in the corner?

"Raaa!" A big black shape jumped
on Henry, knocked him down, and
snatched the chocolate.

Nick's dad burst in.

"Rigoletto! Give that back!" said
Nick's dad, yanking the chocolate out
of the dog's mouth.

"Sorry about that, Henry," he said,
offering it back to Henry.

"Uhh, maybe later," said Henry.

"Okay," said Nick's dad, putting
the slobbery chocolate back in the
cabinet.

Eeew, gross, thought Horrid Henry.

"I love you, Henwy," came a lisping
voice behind him.

"AH HA HA HA HA HA HA HA!"
warbled a high, piercing voice from the
sitting room.

Henry held his ears. Would the
windows shatter?

"Encore!" shrieked the opera karaoke
club.

"Will you marry with me?" asked
Lisping Lily.

"Let's get out of here," said Horrid Henry.

Horrid Henry leaped on Nick's bed.

Yippee, thought Horrid Henry. Time to get bouncing.

Bounce—

Crash!

The bed collapsed in a heap.

"What happened?" said Henry. "I hardly did anything."

"Oh, I broke the bed ages ago," said Nick. "Dad said he was tired of fixing it."

Rats, thought Henry. What a lazy dad.

"How about a pillow fight?" said Henry.

"No pillows," said Nick. "The dogs chewed them."

Hmmm.

They *could* sneak down and raid the freezer, but for some reason Henry didn't really want to go back into that kitchen.

"I know!" said Henry. "Let's watch TV."

"Sure," said New Nick.

"Where is the TV?" said Henry.

"In the living room," said Nick.

"But—the karaoke," said Henry.

"Oh, they won't mind," said Nick. "They're used to noise in this house."

"DUM DUM DE DUM DUMM DUMM

DUM DE DUM DUMM DUMM–"

Horrid Henry sat with his face pressed to the TV. He couldn't hear a word Mutant Max was shrieking with all that racket in the background.

"Maybe we should go to bed," said Horrid Henry, sighing. Anything to get away from the noise.

"Okay," said New Nick.

Phew, thought Horrid Henry. Peace at last.

★ ★ ★

SNORE! SNORE!

Horrid Henry turned over in his
sleeping bag and tried to get comfortable.
He hated sleeping on the floor. He hated
sleeping with the window open. He
hated sleeping with the radio on.

221

And he hated sleeping in the same room with someone who snored.

Awhooooooo! howled the winter wind through the open window.

SNORE! SNORE!

"I'm just a lonesome cowboy, lookin' for a lonesome cowgirl," blared the radio.

WOOF WOOF WOOF barked the dogs.

"Yeowwww!" squealed Henry, as five wet, smelly dogs pounced on him.

"Awhoooo!" howled the wind.

SNORE! SNORE!

"TOREADOR—on guard!" boomed
the opera karaoke downstairs.

Horrid Henry loved noise. But this
was—too much.

He'd have to find somewhere else to
sleep.

Horrid Henry flung open the
bedroom door.

"I love you Henwy," said Lisping Lily.

Slam! Horrid Henry shut the bedroom door.

Horrid Henry did not move.

Horrid Henry did not breathe.

Then he opened the door a fraction.

"Will you marry with me, Henwy?"

Aaarrrgh!!!

Horrid Henry ran from the bedroom and barricaded himself in the linen closet. He settled down on a pile of towels.

Phew. Safe at last.

"I want to give you a big kiss, Henwy," came a little voice beside him.

NOOOOOOOO!

It was three a.m.

"TRA LA LA BOOM-DY AY!"

"—LONESOME COWBOY!"

SNORE! SNORE!

AWHOOOOOOOOOOOOOO!

WOOF! WOOF! WOOF!

Horrid Henry crept to the hall phone and dialed his number.

Dad answered.

"I'm so sorry about Henry, do you want us to come and get him?" Dad mumbled.

"Yes," wailed Horrid Henry. "I need my rest!"

And now it's time for some fun! Let's get started!

TreaSure HuNt

Horrid Henry wants to be a pirate. Draw a line through
the maze to help Horrid Henry find the pirate's treasure!

Horrid Henry's Jokes

Why are zombies never lonely?

They can always dig up a few friends.

What do you call a Tyrannosaurus Rex that sleeps all day?

A dino-snore.

Margaret: Knock knock.

Susan: Who's there?

Margaret: Nun.

Susan: Nun who?

Margaret: Nun of your business.

write your favorite joke here:

_____

_____

_____

Draw a picture to go along with your joke.

You can make your own GLOP!

It's very simple to make your own disgusting, gooey, gross Glop. You can make Glop with anything you can find in the kitchen—the yuckier the better! Horrid Henry and Moody Margaret mixed oatmeal, vinegar, baked beans, moldy cheese, and even peanut butter into their icky Glop. If you want to make some simple Glop, try this basic recipe.

Ingredients

16 oz box of cornstarch

1 ½ cups water

Food coloring (optional)

Directions

Dump the cornstarch and water into a large bowl. Add about 15 or 20 drops of food coloring. Squish the Glop together with your hands until it's all mixed. Now gross out your little brother or sister by letting the Glop ooze through your fingers! Yuck!

What will you put in your Glop? Horrid Henry's rules are to use only things you can find in the kitchen. On the lines below, write all the gross things you could use to make your Glop.

_____

_____

_____

_____

_____

_____

_____

_____

_____

_____

My ~~Horrid Henry's~~ Time Machine

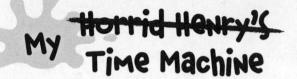

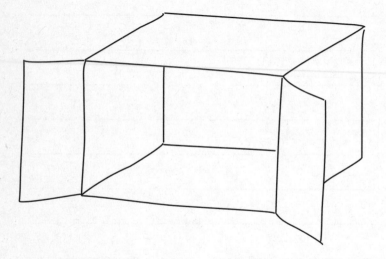

In *Horrid Henry and the Mega-Mean Time Machine* Henry makes a time machine out of a big box. In the space above, draw your own time machine. What time would you visit in your Mega-Mean Time Machine? What would you do?

_____

_____

Solve the Riddle!

First, write the answer to the math problem on the line. Then, using the Key, find the letter that matches the number. Write the letter in the box. When all the boxes are filled in, they will spell out the answer to the riddle!

13 + 8 = _21_ ⬜T

11 + 11 = ___ ⬜

3 + 7 = ___ ⬜

20 + 6 = ___ ⬜

15 - 5 = ___ ⬜

4 + 8 = ___ ⬜

30 - 4 = ___ ⬜

40 - 26 = ___ ⬜

1 + 9 = ___ ⬜

7 + 5 = ___ ⬜

WHERE DO SKELETONS SWIM?

_____
Write the answer here

KEY:

A	B	C	D	E	F	G	H	I	J	K	L	M
12	24	3	26	10	18	7	22	15	1	20	11	25

N	O	P	Q	R	S	T	U	V	W	X	Y	Z
5	17	8	19	2	14	21	9	16	4	23	13	6

Word Match

An adjective is a word used to describe a person, place, or thing. All of the children in the Horrid Henry series have an adjective before their name that starts with the same letter as their name. Can you match up the characters with their adjectives? The first one is done for you:

HORRID	ANDREW
PERFECT	DAVE
MOODY	PETER
RUDE	SUSAN
DIZZY	HENRY
SOUR	BRIAN
LAZY	MARGARET
ANXIOUS	RALPH
CLEVER	LINDA
BRAINY	CLARE

Now that you've matched up all of the Horrid Henry characters, write your Horrid Henry name below. Remember, the first letter of your adjective should be the same as the first letter of your name!

My Horrid Henry name is:

_____   _____

Even more jokes!

Why do elephants have gray trunks?

They're all on the same swimming team.

What do you call a flying skunk?

A smellicopter.

Why is the letter V like a monster?

It comes after U.

Coloring Fun!

Horrid Henry

Coloring Fun!

Moody Margaret and Sour Susan

My Favorite Books!

What is your favorite book that you have read in school?

_____

What is your favorite book to read at home?

_____

Who do you talk to about your favorite books?

_____

_____

_____

_____

_____

_____

Draw your own
Horrid Henry book cover!

Pick one of the stories in this book and draw your
own book cover for it.

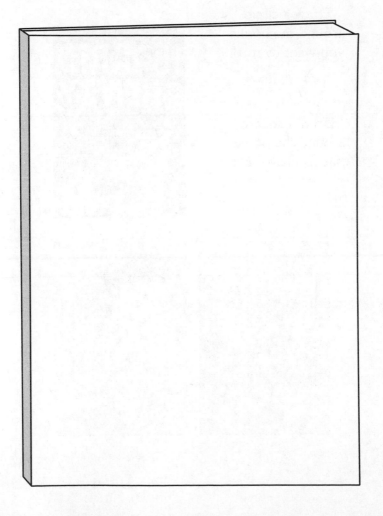

Have you read all the Horrid Henry books?

Draw a circle around the books you want to read.

Draw a square around the books that you have read.

About the Author

Photo: Francesco Guidicini

Francesca Simon spent her childhood on the beach in California and then went to Yale and Oxford Universities to study medieval history and literature. She now lives in London with her family. She has written over forty-five books and won the Children's Book of the Year in 2008 at the Galaxy British Book Awards for *Horrid Henry and the Abominable Snowman*.